Rules of the Road

Joan Bauer was born in Illinois, and is a freelance writer who has worked in advertising, radio, television, and film. Her first novel, *Squashed*, has been very well received both here and in the USA. She now lives in Darien, Connecticut, with her husband, daughter, and assorted animals.

Also by Joan Bauer
Squashed
Thwonk

Rules of the Road

JOAN BAUER

Orion Children's Books
and

Dolphin Paperbacks

For Jean, with love

With abundant thanks to George Nicholson,
who led the way,
and to Betsy Barker,
who taught me about Texas.

First published in Great Britain in 1999
as a Dolphin paperback
by Orion Children's Books
a division of the Orion Publishing Group Ltd
Orion House
5 Upper St Martin's Lane
London WC2H 9EA

A catalogue record for this book
is available from the British Library

Typeset at The Spartan Press Ltd,
Lymington, Hants

Printed in Great Britain by
Clays Ltd, St Ives plc.

ISBN 1 85881 648 3 (pb)

One

I LEAPED ONTO THE SLIDING LADDER IN THE BACK room of Gladstone's Shoe Store of Chicago, gave it a shove, and glided fast towards the end of the floor-to-ceiling shelves of shoeboxes. My keen retailer's eye found the chocolate-brown loafers, size 13, I slid the ladder to the Nikes, grabbed two boxes of easy walkers (white and beige) size 4½ narrow, pushed again to women's saddles, found the waxhides, size 7, rode the ladder to the door one-handed. Children, do not try this at home. I am a shoe professional. I jumped off as Murray Castlebaum, my boss, rushed past me.

'It's a madhouse out there, kid.' Murray grinned, rifling through shoeboxes.

We love it when it gets busy.

I walked quickly back on the sales floor, made eye contact with each of my customers so they'd know I cared. Every movement counts when you're selling shoes, especially when the store fills up with customers. You look at people calmly; you let them know you'll take care of them – you're not panicked even though people are holding up shoes and barking sizes at you all at once. I just remember what Murray told me: people want to know someone's for them. I've sold lots of shoes this way.

The tired woman with the three screaming boys tried on the waxhide saddles.

'Mommy, I want to go!' cried the youngest boy and the

other two chimed in. This could blow my sale because she was outnumbered. I took out my stopwatch that I used for emergencies, handed it to the oldest boy.

'Breath-holding contest,' I directed. 'The winner gets striped laces. Best two out of three.'

'Cool.' The boys started holding their breath, mere putty in my hands. The woman looked at me gratefully, freed to shop.

I raced to the older man, slid the loafers on his bony feet, felt the toe. His face went soft. I smiled. These shoes sell themselves. He stood up, did a little dancing movement.

Moved to the woman with the dangling Siamese earrings, the pouncing cat pin. Slipped the Nikes on her fat foot, mentioned the tri-density compression plug midsole that would energize her feet on pavement, told her to give them a good test. Circled back around like a good sheepdog, keeping watch.

'How are those feeling?' I asked Cat Woman, who grinned.

Showed the older man the hand-stitching and richly grained texture on his loafers.

Pointed out the classic, yet fresh appeal of the waxhide saddle.

The woman nodded as her boys argued over who won the contest – she'd take the shoes.

The older man took out his wallet. 'I'll take them, miss.'

A yes from Cat Woman.

The woman with the toddler I'd waited on earlier bought three pairs of baby sandals in white, pink, and dress black.

They can't say no.

I walked my customers to the counter, thanked each one, tallied up the five per cent commission in my head, keeping my eye on the man and the little girl who just walked in. Murray pushed back his three strands of hair that he tried to comb over his balding head and did his dead chicken imitation, stretching his neck long, bugging his eyes out. This meant I wait on the man and girl. I headed towards them, stepping lightly.

'So what are you doing in school these days, Becky?' the man asked the little girl.

'Daddy,' she said, 'I already told you last week.'

The man checked his watch. A weekend father, probably. Be thankful, Becky. At least yours comes around.

Becky tried on pink ballet slippers, white cowgirl boots, and black patent leathers.

She got them all.

I walked Becky and her dad to the counter.

'Listen,' the father said as he flipped out his Visa card. 'I'm going to have to take you back early today, Beck. I've got an appointment.'

My dad used to say that to me on the rare occasion that he came around.

I handed her a balloon and told her how great she's going to look in her new shoes.

Becky stared at the children's shoe display I arranged. Murray said it was my best one yet. It had stuffed clown dolls and circus stickers and a wind-up trapeze toy that moved across a wire. The kids always ran to it whenever they came into the store. Becky walked to the display, her little face caved in, watching as the toy man buzzed across the wire above the sneakers.

I wanted to tell her I understood. I walked over to her, put my hand on her shoulder, and settled for one of those looks that passed between strangers. Her father checked his watch again, rushed her out the door.

Mrs Madeline Gladstone, the supremely aged president of Gladstone's Shoes (176 outlets in 37 states; corporate offices in Dallas, Texas), stood by the cash register under the large white five-pointed Lone Star of Texas that was the symbol of Gladstone's Shoe Stores everywhere. She came to our store every day when she was in town. Mrs Gladstone had houses in Dallas and Chicago, but lately she'd been spending all her time here. She was very short but made up for it like one of those little yippy dogs who barks at anything. She ran her fingers through her coarse white hair, made notes on a pad inside a blue leather folder marked 'personal.' Some people just naturally make you nervous. She was retiring this year, handing the business over to her son, Elden. Murray said retiring was probably going to kill her because the shoe business had been her whole life. It didn't help that Elden was pond scum.

He came to the store three months ago, saying how the shoe business was changing and we were going to get new lower-priced merchandise that was going to fly off the shelves. The merchandise came, but it never made it on the shelves. It looked good on the outside, but Murray Castlebaum's got X-ray vision. He looked past the brushed leather and the fancy labels to the thinner soles and the wider stitching and the second-rate lining. Then Murray shoved everything in the closet and stood on the ladder in the back room and gave a misty-eyed speech about how you've got to live what you sell and he wasn't about to start living with garbage.

Most people think selling shoes is pretty ho-hum, but if you hang with shoe people long enough you plug into the high drama.

I looked around. The crowd had cleared. Customers come in swarms, like locusts.

'Break, kid.'

Murray motioned me to the back room. I was fifteen and a half when I started at Gladstone's last year, sopho-more year, the year of the Big Slump. I gained seventeen and a half pounds. I went from centre forward to second-string guard on the girls basketball team because I just can't jump. I got a C minus in History, which knocked me off the honour roll because my history teacher didn't like my essays or my end-of-the-year term paper ('Our Shoes, Ourselves – Footwear Through the Ages'). I became the brunt of Billy Mundy's mean jokes until I shoved him against the wall when he called me '*Ms* Moose' for the zillionth time, told him I'd rip his left kidney out if he said that again. I just limped through sophomore year, all five feet eleven inches of me, wondering why God had invented adolescence.

But there was Gladstone's.

I succeeded here. I made money here. I didn't feel big, awkward, and lost. I felt successful. I helped people. They looked to me instead of away. I couldn't wait to come here after school, couldn't wait to head out to work early on Saturday mornings. My grandmother always said that everyone needs something in life that they do pretty well. For me, it's selling shoes.

Still, I nearly collapsed during those first weeks wondering how I was going to remember everything. But you know how it is when you start something new; you mess up for a while and then gradually you find the rhythm. Murray Castlebaum's a good, patient boss except when his diverticulitis acts up and then you steer clear because the man becomes Frankenstein, or Frankenbaum, as I call him. At the end of each week, Murray asks me, 'OK, kid, what did you learn?' At first I'd just shrug and say something about handling customers better, but Murray didn't like that because he'd been selling shoes for twenty-three years and figured something big should have rubbed off.

'The number one thing you gotta know to sell shoes,' Murray said, 'is that every shoe has a story. You know how it's made, you know how to sell it.'

So I made it my business to know what was good and bad about each shoe. You can put four pairs of sandals in front of me and I can tell you which one to wear on the beach, which one to wear for a walk, which one to buy for the long haul, and which one to avoid altogether. And when it comes to selling sneakers you better have done your homework or you'll get blown out of the water. You sell road traction and heel alignment, and don't let anyone tell you that a multiple sports-trainer is going to give you the strength of a long-distance runner. It's a bold new shoe world out there and not everyone knows how to compete.

I sat on the folding chair by the helium tank and the boxes of Gladstone's Shoe Store balloons with the Texas star that were blown up and given to every child who walked through the door. I turned the helium gauge on, took a quick gulp of funny gas, and squeaked out, 'Cat Woman lives.'

'Watch the gas,' Murray said to me, looking through boxes of loafers.

I let loose a high-pitched helium giggle, opened my purse, and took out what had become my most prized possession.

There it was, nestled between my Chicago Public Library card and my Red Cross CPR certificate – my own, personal driver's licence – six months old today.

Jenna Boller

Eyes: Brown

Hair: Red

Height: 5'11"

Weight: None of your business

An official Illinois driver.

If only the photo wasn't so awful – my flat nose looked flatter, my round face looked like a globe, my auburn hair hung frizzed and heavy on my shoulders like too much fur. My dark eyes (one of my best features) looked guilty.

My sister got the beauty in the family. I got the personality.

I held up my licence and chirped out, 'My passport to new worlds, Murray. Adventure. Romance. Freedom.'

'The romance dies, kid, the first time you're wedged between two Mack trucks at rush hour on the Eisenhower Expressway.'

Murray lumbered out as I cradled my licence. I was a good driver, everyone said so. Cars never scared me. I had respect for their power, but I worked hard to learn the rules.

My big plan at the end of the summer, after clocking in many full-time hours at Gladstone's, is to buy a car – a red one – with a sunroof and leather buckets. Then, I'm going to explore all of Illinois, and then Wisconsin, and then—

'Where's my Jenna girl?'

I froze at the voice coming from the sales floor.

It couldn't be.

'Jenna girl, this is your father calling you!'

I looked for a place to hide. There was no back door.

'Sir . . .' It was Murray's voice. 'We can't have you—'

'I'm here, sir,' my father announced, drunk, 'to see my daughter.'

I couldn't move. Murray, bless him, said, 'She's gone for the day.'

'Now don't give me that now.' My father swirled the words together. 'Just want to see her for a little minute. Haven't seen her for a long time, very long.'

Two years and seven months, to be exact. But who's counting?

Not me. Not any more. I used to count the letters I sent him that he never answered, the presents I mailed on his birthday and Christmas.

I got up from the stool like I was dragging lead weights. I could get another job after they fired me. I was a good worker, everyone said so. I could sell anything to any-body. I stood at the door and watched my father in dirty jeans and an old golf shirt and grubby sneakers scratch his head and fall into a plaid chair as Mrs Gladstone snapped her long, bony fingers at Murray to *do something*.

'Jenna girl! You got tall there.' His cloudy eyes tried to focus.

Please, God, let the helium have worn off. I said, 'It happens,' but I still sounded like a cartoon mouse.

I walked up to Mrs Gladstone, could smell her light perfume wafting up from her navy blue pin-striped suit. No customers in the store. That was something. I looked her straight in the eye, tried to aim my voice low.

'I'm sorry about this, Mrs Gladstone. I'll take care of it.' Better, but still Disney.

Her grey eyes blasted through me. She stood rigidly erect, every thick, snowy curl in place.

My face sizzled hot. I walked slowly towards my father, not looking at the mirrors on the blue walls on either side of me, not looking at the white sign above the door, WE'RE NOT JUST SELLING SHOES, WE'RE SELLING QUALITY. I looked at the blue carpet with the white stars, took my father's arm to lead him out of the store, onto the street, somewhere, anywhere but here.

'Did you miss your old man?'

I led him out to Wabash Street, underneath the elevated train tracks. Dad was never a mean drunk, you could put him places, lean him against things and he'd pretty much stay put. That helped when I was smaller and I had to put him places when Mom had had enough.

I arranged him on the station steps, put his hands together to grip the rail. I was really glad that I was one of those people who had delayed reactions to trauma.

'Well,' he blubbered, 'watcha been doing?'

An El train barrelled by overhead, shaking the street.

Steel scraping steel, the train screeched around the corner. I gave him two years and seven months worth. 'Stuff, you know.' The gas had worn off. I'm definitely off helium for good.

'Me too.' He swayed down on the steps as two old women moved quickly past us. 'You probably think I'm drunk, Jenna girl, but I'm not.'

'Really.' He always called me 'Jenna girl' when he was plastered.

'I'm on medication that makes me . . . funny.'

I focused in hard at the Lemmy's hot dog poster (steaming dog with everything, including grilled onions) so I wouldn't have to look at my father or see the staring people looking at me like I'm some poor, pitiful case.

Drunken Dad Disgraces Daughter.

We stayed there for a while not saying anything. When I was nine, Mom had sent me to a therapist, Ms Lynch, after she and Dad got divorced so I'd have a place to yell and scream, which I never did. Ms Lynch had a puppet, a brown furry chipmunk named Chester, that I'd put on my hand and tell him the story of my dad's alcoholism and how I'd never known if he was going to be a good dad one day or a bad one. One time, Ms Lynch made Chester's voice and said it was OK if I got angry. I got angry all right, but not at Chester. I told Ms Lynch that Chester was a chipmunk and *didn't* talk. Then I told her I knew that storks didn't bring babies so stop trying to snow me.

Dumb as it seems, I could have used Chester now.

'I'm going to have to get back to work, Dad.' I said this low, mature.

Dad belched. He was wearing the Timex watch I'd sent him last Christmas. Nice to know it arrived.

'Jus wanted to see you, honey. I meant to call.'

He always said that.

'Yeah. I know.'

I felt the armour going over my heart and mind, the steel rod shooting through my back. I didn't ask where he was working now. The jobs never lasted long. He was always selling something – aluminium siding, screen doors, toasters, used cars – I got my gift for selling from him, that's what people said. He had a brief stint as a door-to-door vacuum cleaner salesman; kept a ball of dirt in his pocket to throw on the carpet when the front door opened; got bit bad by an irritated pit bull who didn't appreciate the Eureka suction. Part of me wanted to walk away and leave him there, the other part couldn't. I'd worked hard at seeing his alcoholism as a disease he was stuck in. Love the person, hate the bad things they do. Sometimes loving from far off is a whole lot easier than eyeball to eyeball.

'Is there someplace you're staying, Dad? Someplace you need to get to?'

He tried standing up to reach in his pocket, fumbled badly, finally pulled a matchbook out, opened the cover, handed it to me. 'Sueann Turnbolt, 1260 Wells Street, 555-4286,' it read.

Another girlfriend probably.

'Is she there now, Dad?'

'S'waiting for me.'

Mr Romance. I hailed a cab, got him inside, gave the driver ten dollars and the address. 'We can get together when I'm not working, Dad.'

'Okey dokey, Jenna girl.'

I shut the cab door and watched it head down the street. I felt exhausted, like I hadn't slept for days.

Daddy's home.

The last time he showed up was when I was a freshman. I was walking home from school with my friends and he pulled up in a broken-down Dodge, jumped out with a big toothy smile like I should have been expecting him all along. Dad always made an entrance.

He hung around town that summer, drinking, not drinking, making promises, breaking them.

Daddy's home.

I leaned against the elevated train stairway, closed my eyes, threw back my head.

I didn't know if I could handle it this time.

Two

KEEP GOING.
I ran back to Gladstone's Shoes pushing aside pain and anger. Murray said customers are like wild animals – they can tell when you're upset and they'll use it against you.

Smile.

A few people in the store, but Murray was handling it. Mrs Gladstone was studying the Johnston and Murphy display like it held the secret to life. Maybe I could tiptoe around her into the—

'Your father,' said Mrs Gladstone in her soft Texas drawl, 'is quite a—'

My body clenched. 'I'm sorry about him, ma'am. If you don't want me to work here any more, I'll understand.'

Mrs Gladstone folded her skinny arms across her chest. I was toast.

I would not fall apart if I got fired.

I'd just take my stuff and go.

'What manure,' she spat.

I guess I wasn't fired.

'Why would I penalize you for something that is clearly your father's problem?' She stood there waiting.

'Well . . .'

What could I say to her?

What could I say to anyone?

My father has had this problem all my life and if I had

one wish in this world it would be that he could beat it.

But you know how it is with wishes. Some you catch, and others are like trying to grab Jello.

Mom's note on the dining room table to me and Faith read:

> Daughters of mine,
> In case you haven't noticed, no one has seen the top of our dining room table in months. I seem to recall it is oak, but as the days dwindle by, I'm less and less sure. Perhaps this is because your school books, files, papers, magazines, letters, underwear, etc., are shielding it from normal use. My goal for you, dear offspring, to be accomplished in twenty-four hours (no excuses), is the clearing/exhuming of this space so that we may gather around it once again and spend quality time. Even though I am working the night shift, I will still be watching. Do it or die.
> Your loving mother

My younger sister Faith padded in, holding a box of extra-heavy garbage bags. At fourteen, Faith was beautiful beyond knowing – blonde, green-eyed, finely cut cheekbones – an example of what God could do if he was paying attention. It used to bug me that she got all the gorgeous genes, but like my grandmother always said, there's a downside to everything. I can walk into a room looking like I've slept in a torture chamber with poisonous snakes, and people mostly ignore it. But when Faith looks bad, she's got a crowd around her telling her about it.

'You want the front half or the back?' she asked, turning up her perfect nose at the table. Faith always seemed put together – her head matched her neck; her long legs matched the rest of her body. I felt like I'd been glued together with surplus parts – my shoulders were big and boxy, my legs were long and skinny. I had a swan-thin neck that held my round head in place.

I studied the table to figure out which half had the least work. 'If we split it lengthwise down the middle,' I said, 'you take the one closest to you—'

'That's got more stuff, Jenna!'

Precisely.

'I saw Dad.'

Faith sat down. 'You did?'

I told her.

'Oh, Jenna, you must have been mortified!'

'It hasn't hit me yet.'

Faith fidgeted on the chair. She tugged at her long ponytail. 'Did he mention me?'

'Yeah. Of course.' He hadn't.

'Well . . . what did he say?'

'He misses you and wishes he could have come around more and wonders how you're doing.'

I always told her this. There's a responsibility that comes with being a big sister. I guess she believed me, although you can't always tell with Faith. Last Father's Day she was storming around the house, slamming doors, telling everyone to buzz off, she was *fine*. Father's Day is my least favourite holiday. I can never find the right card. I can't send the 'Dad, I can always count on you' ones; I nix 'Thanks for everything' and 'You're the greatest.' What the world needs is an alternative card: 'Dad, I love you, even though you haven't been there for me.'

Faith lifted a stack of fashion magazines from the table like they weighed six tons. She is probably going to become a model someday even though I warned her that smiling and twirling under hot lights has been medically proven to cause shallowness. I think it's fine to look the best you can, but when that's the biggest thing you concentrate on, you can miss the fun of life's grungier moments like hanging around in men's pyjamas, eating pork fried rice from the carton with chopsticks, and not caring how much gets ground in the rug.

'Do you think he does miss us?' Faith asked.

'I think he's got a disease, Faith, that keeps him from being the person he could be.' I learned this when I went to Al-Anon, a group that helps families of alcoholics. Faith didn't go. 'Faith is handling things,' Mom explained. 'She doesn't have the memories you do, Jenna. She was so young when your dad and I divorced.' It made me feel like some big infected boil that needed lancing. Faith always got off easy.

Faith looked at the cover of *Vogue* sadly. 'Do you think he ever misses us, Jenna? I mean *really?*'

I grabbed a garbage bag. 'I don't know.'

'If he really cared about us, he'd stop drinking.'

'It's not that easy.'

'Well, don't you think I know that, Jenna? What do you think I am, some moron?'

Faith flung her hand across a corner of the table, knocked my personal pile of *Travel and Leisure* magazines on the floor, ran into her room, and slammed the door.

Part of me felt like kicking in her door, telling her to grow up. It wasn't my fault she never saw Dad. It's not like she was missing much. Everyone loses when Dad comes back.

I knelt down to pick up the travel magazines, knocked one off the top with an article about Texas. 'Everything is Bigger in Texas' the headline read. I threw it at Faith's closed door.

'I don't think you're a moron,' I shouted as Faith's sobs filled the apartment.

I was standing at the stove, having just flipped my world-class grilled mozzarella and tomato sandwich in the pan. It was perfectly brown on one side, the mozzarella cheese was melting and oozing from between the seven grain bread. Ooze was the whole point of a grilled cheese sandwich – my grandmother taught me that.

I read my mother's note that she had taped over the sink of dirty dishes:

> Someone wash these. It doesn't matter who. What matters is that when I return home after ten hours on my feet patching up emergency patients that I will not see the pot roast pan from four days ago with petrified gravy still on it. Make no mistake about it – this is a test.

It was signed, 'YLM' for Your Loving Mother. Mom is an emergency-room nurse at St Joseph's Hospital and is working the night shift for the time and a half pay. We don't see her much, which is hard, but Mom's schedule is toughest on Faith. She needs more of Mom's time than I do. Faith is at that age where she hasn't seen enough of the world to know she can handle herself.

Mom works hard to spend time with each of us. She and I like to take long walks together all around Chicago – being Type A personalities, we do our best talking when we're moving. The thing we've got most in common is our independent streak – we know how to take care of ourselves and we like being on our own. But sometimes my mother goes into guilt overdrive. Saying how she should have been tougher on Dad and left him sooner. Then she tries to make up for everything in my life that she thinks made me the social zero that I am today.

Wouldn't you like to have a big party? she asks. I know we didn't have your friends over much when you were younger, but parties are a good way to get to know more people.

Not really, Mom. I don't like crowds much.

Maybe you should go to ballroom dancing class, Jenna.

—— 16 ——

Having social dancing skills is always important later in life.

The boys come up to my armpits, Mom.

Maybe you shouldn't work such long hours, honey. I'd like you to have time to just be a teenager.

I'm trying to make money, Mother. I like selling shoes.

I'm more like my dad than my mom. That used to scare me because I thought it meant I'd end up like him. But Grandma sat me down and said how God had managed to give me the best parts of my father (his sales ability, his business sense) without all the tragedy.

I studied my sandwich in the pan. It had achieved perfection. I put it on a plate with red grapes and dill pickles, counted fifteen seconds, the exact amount of time to wait before biting into a grilled cheese without burning the roof of my sensitive teenage mouth.

The phone rang. I waited two rings, three. Faith, the phone queen, wasn't getting it, which meant she was still having her snit. Four rings. I grabbed it.

'Hello?'

'Jenna Boller, if you please,' said the familiar southern voice.

'Speaking.'

'This is Madeline Gladstone.'

I stood at attention.

'Are you there?' she asked.

'Yes, ma'am.'

I racked my brain.

I locked the storage closet before I left today, counted the money. Murray took it to the bank.

'Is everything OK at the store, Mrs Gladstone?'

'It is.'

I waited.

'I have a proposal for you.'

'You do?'

'You drive? I assume.'

'You mean like a car?'

'That was the concept, yes.'

'I've had my licence for six months.'

'You drive properly?'

'I guess . . . I mean . . . yes.'

Faith had just come into the kitchen to forage for food. She was opening and closing doors, shaking Tupperware containers. She was doing this while practising model poses and expressions. Fashion models don't smile much. They get paid to look like someone just pinched them from behind. Faith saw my grilled cheese, started towards it. I grabbed the plate, held it over my head. Faith tried grabbing it, but she's only five eight. I had three inches on her. Grandma always said it's a blessing to be tall.

'Come to my home tomorrow morning at seven o'clock, Jenna. You can drive me downtown in my Cadillac. After that we'll see.'

'I don't understand.'

Mrs Gladstone sighed. 'I need a driver.'

'A driver . . .?'

This was a full-fledged disaster waiting to happen. She gave me her address on Astor Street.

'Mrs Gladstone, I've only driven a twelve-year-old Honda Civic, never a *Cadillac*.'

'That will change tomorrow, won't it? Good night.'

'But—'

Click.

I felt the colour drain from my face. I put the plate down.

'Who was that?' Faith asked.

I hung up the receiver, sat down on the wobbly stool by the sink. 'I've never driven a Cadillac.'

'You've never been in a Cadillac,' Faith countered, grabbing half my sandwich.

Morning. Five forty-four.

I lay in bed looking at the ceiling; a spider's web hung between the corners, camouflaged against my ivory walls. A fly buzzed around it.

'Stupid,' I said to the fly, 'you're going to be brunch.'

The fly buzzed closer to the web, too close. He struggled against the sticky threads. The spider came down from a string on the ceiling.

Any last words, fly?

The spider watched the fly until it stopped moving, then dug in.

Life and death played out before my very eyes.

You don't see these things if you clean your room regularly.

Five fifty-five. The alarm blared. I turned it off, eased my numb self up. Headed for the shower, wondering if Dad made it to Sueann's; rounded the picture wall of family photo memories.

Mom glaring at a roasted pig at a Hawaiian luau.

Faith modelling a surgical pants suit at a hospital charity luncheon.

Me at the beach, submerged in sand from the neck down, "Beware of Teen" written across my stomach.

My grandmother, like I always remember her – bent over her Singer sewing machine, bright fabric everywhere. The photo was taken in her tailor shop on Clark Street before she was diagnosed with the Alzheimer's disease that took piece after piece of her memory until her old self was all but gone.

Grandma was my best friend. She understood everything about me – how serious I could get, how hard I worked at my part-time jobs. When I was twelve I won the *Chicago Tribune* "Blood and Guts Award" for selling more daily and Sunday subscriptions than any paper kid in the city or suburbs. Grandma said she always knew I was going to win something big. She took me out to dinner at Wok World, my favourite Chinese restaurant, and stuck my winner's plaque right on the table by the low salt soy sauce.

Two years ago Mom and I brought her to a nursing home. It was one of the hardest things I've ever had to do. Faith rode with us in the car for two blocks, but she couldn't handle watching Grandma just stare out the window. Faith jumped out at North Avenue and ran home crying.

I visit Grandma at the home. Take the 151 bus up Sheridan Road past Belmont Harbour to Shady Oaks Nursing Home where she lives. Her roommate Gladys always remembers me. Grandma remembers me sometimes. Mostly she remembers how I used to visit her when she lived in Wisconsin when I was small.

I bring her flowers sometimes. Daisies are her favourites. I used to read to her from the newspaper, but she got depressed at how bad the world has gotten. Mostly I just sit with her and smile when she looks at me with her scared eyes. I tell her how when I get my own car I'm going to take her for a ride and we'll have a picnic with fried chicken and lemon cookies like we used to when I was little. Then I stand by the memory board I made her. It's a bulletin board with "I love you, Grandma" across the top in red felt letters. Below are photographs of me, Mom, and Faith, pieces of fabric like she had in her shop, a few postcards of Chicago, the satin ribbon she braided my hair with when I graduated from eighth grade, her huge flowered hat that she'd wear to church on Sundays. She goes up and touches the board sometimes, particularly the fabric; rolls the tweeds and silks between her fingers and for that moment she seems connected. Before the Alzheimer's got really bad she said to me, 'Jenna Louise Boller, I'm counting on you. As this thing gets worse, you're going to have to help me remember.'

If I were God I would wipe out every disease in the world beginning with the A's: AIDS, Alcoholism, Alzheimer's . . .

Three

*I*T WAS 6:56 AM. A FINE SUMMER MIST COVERED the expensive brownstones on Astor Street. I never got to talk to my mom about Dad or Mrs Gladstone or what a person needed to know to be the driver of a demanding rich person. I was extra loud in the kitchen making my breakfast to hopefully wake my mother up, but there are just so many times you can drop a stainless steel bowl without seeming suspicious and Mom slept through all of it. I thought of all the good drivers I'd ever seen, and I couldn't for the life of me figure out what made them that way. They just got behind the wheel, drove, and didn't run into things. The not running into things was important.

I stood in front of Mrs Gladstone's ritzy three-story brownstone building. It was surrounded by pink and white azalea bushes and a black and bronze fence. I was wearing my khaki suit and my stacked heel leather shoes that were very good for driving. I pulled back the gold lion door knocker, gave it a ram.

A curly haired woman in a black maid's uniform opened it.

'I'm Jenna,' I said, smoothing down my hair that had reached warp-frizz.

She looked me up and down, uncertain, then led me into a hallway that was filled with things that looked old and expensive. The wallpaper had gold peacocks and thick stripes, a grandfather's clock with gold around the edges bonged seven rings.

'I appreciate promptness.' Mrs Gladstone walked slowly down a spiral wooden staircase like a queen. She stepped onto a fat oriental rug. Her grey eyes studied me. A huge oil painting that looked like Mrs Gladstone in better days hung over the fireplace the next room over.

This was not a place where you hunker down and have a grilled cheese.

'And what do you think is the most important qualification for being a good driver?' She asked this like we'd been talking for a while.

'Well . . .' I almost said luck, but that seemed irresponsible.

'Come now. A person with a six-month-old licence should have an opinion.'

Six months and a day. 'Focus,' I said loud and clear, which surprised me.

Mrs Gladstone's face registered mild appreciation. 'My late husband, Floyd, always said that the mark of a man was his ability to focus.'

'My grandfather said if you weren't watching the knife you could hack off your thumb.' She looked at me strangely. 'He was a butcher,' I added.

She laughed, the good kind from the heart, and motioned me to a door. 'It's time you met the car.'

'I'd love to meet him. I mean . . . . *her.*'

'Believe me, I'm not that attached to it.'

I groaned inside and followed her down the stairs.

'Floyd always said that a Cadillac offered the world's purest driving experience.'

We were standing in the garage by the car – a white, spotless beast of a thing with a hood ornament and blue leather interior. I kicked the steel-belted radials like I knew what I was doing. The car was pointed away from the garage door, which meant that to get the car out, I would have to back it up. I was a C-minus backer-upper.

'A Cadillac, Floyd always said, is entirely trustworthy. It has been tested in any and all conditions and will perform to the utmost to protect its driver.'

Was this a car or a Seeing Eye dog?

Mrs Gladstone handed me the car keys like they opened the gates of heaven. I unlocked the driver door, started to get in.

'A driver *always* lets the passenger in first.'

'Right.'

I got out, slammed the door shut.

'And don't slam the door. This *isn't* a truck.'

'Sorry.'

I let Mrs Gladstone in the back and gently shut the door like it was holy. Mrs Gladstone nodded to me, which I guess meant I could now get inside the car. I squeezed behind the wheel. Mrs Gladstone pointed at a button near the dashboard. I pressed it. My seat adjusted perfectly.

I checked the mirrors, the dashboard monitor, buckled my seat belt. I felt like I was in a tank.

She sniffed. 'Start the motor.'

I fumbled with the key, started the engine, put the car in reverse, and decided not to ask if she was a praying person.

'Here we go,' I said, inching the huge car backwards.

'*Freeze!*' she shrieked.

I slammed on the brake.

'I believe it's customary to open the garage door before backing out of it!'

'Sorry, Mrs Gladstone . . . I'm kind of nervous.'

'Press the button on the controlboard.'

I pressed it. The garage door went up.

'Proceed,' she said stiffly. 'And may God Almighty be merciful.'

'Amen,' I said and slowly backed the white beast up the driveway onto Astor Street.

I inched down the street. Three cab drivers began honking behind me. This was probably because I was going fifteen miles an hour. They could honk their rotten little hearts out for all I cared. I wasn't going any faster. Numbers were blinking on the dashboard: inside/outside temperatures, gas mileage. The cab drivers moved from honking to threatening gestures. I wanted my mother's twelve-year-old Honda. Gas, speedometer, broken radio. Nothing fancy.

'Turn left and take LaSalle Street downtown,' ordered Mrs Gladstone.

I turned left, steered the Cadillac behind a LaSalle Street number 11 bus for protection; it was the only thing on the road bigger than this car. My neck muscles tensed as I gripped the wheel and obeyed all the commands from the back.

'Turn left . . . not there, here.'

'The light has been green for some time now.'

'The driver to your left making those filthy gestures does have the right of way.'

Driving makes you a trusting person. You're on the road with potential dangers everywhere and like an idiot you keep moving forward. Maniacs could be driving next to me and I wouldn't know until they cut me off and propelled me into oncoming traffic. A teenage girl honked loudly and raised an angry fist when I obeyed the law and stopped at a yellow light changing to red. There was no loyalty in my age demographic.

Finally, I pulled the car to the front of Gladstone's Shoes on Wabash Avenue, rolled it over the curb, actually, but at this point, I wasn't going to be picky. We were there. Murray was unlocking the protective chain and fence around the door that guarded the store from nocturnal shoe thugs. Gladstone's always opened at eight AM to get a jump on the competition. He nearly dropped his teeth when he saw us. I smiled my indentured servant smile, got out, gave the door a little tap shut, opened Mrs Gladstone's door, held a hand out for her, helped her up. She told me to pull the car into the twenty-four-hour parking garage where Lorenzo would take care of it. Lorenzo could have it as far as I was concerned. I wanted to say we both had a lot to be thankful for, beginning with the fact that we were still alive.

I stood rigidly as Mrs Gladstone walked past me.

'At ease,' she said, and walked strictly into the store.

I sold shoes like crazy all morning. I did talk one customer out of a sale because the shoes she wanted were all wrong. I never sell just for style, always comfort. If a customer is scrunching up her face, looking miserable in a pair of shoes that she says will probably break in, I tell her no, don't buy them. Your feet will guide you. Listen to your toes. Cordovan leather and pinched tips aren't worth torture. The next time she needs a pair, she'll probably come back to me.

I don't know what it is about selling shoes that I love the most. There's something about the whole experience that brings you closer to people – working with feet that aren't considered the most glamorous part of the body but are one of the most important parts; getting down on your knees to wait on people you'd never meet any other way. Murray Castlebaum said selling shoes is the quickest road to humility in all of retail.

I was going to have lunch with Opal Kincaid, my best friend, who worked in a Fotomat booth on State Street and had to get out regularly or her brain would bake. Opal had a fender bender with her father's new Dodge last week and was grounded until August, except for working (her father got her next six pay cheques as payment) and having lunch with me. She had a huge calendar in her room that she used to mark off the days like a prisoner in solitary confinement. She was standing on the street waiting for me, desperate for teen companionship. I was halfway out the door when Mrs Gladstone grabbed me.

'I've asked Mildred to substitute for you at the store this afternoon,' she announced. 'You will drive me to Evanston.'

Evanston was a near north suburb that required a trip on Lake Shore Drive, a piece of road where people tended to go very fast. Lorenzo pulled the Cadillac in front of the store, got out, and handed me the keys.

'I have a lunch date with my friend, ma'am.'

'Which you will postpone.' Mrs Gladstone marched to the car.

Opal grabbed my arm. 'Tell her you can't go, Jenna. We have *things* to discuss.'

The *things* were boys – Bob Goldblume and Jerry Burgess – Opal's two new crushes. Opal always fell for boys in pairs – if one didn't work out, she had a backup. I've only liked one guy really – Matt Wicks – a seriously intelligent tall senior who (a) did not follow the crowd and (b) did not know I existed. Opal couldn't cope with my dateless state and kept trying to fix me up with sub-par guys like Morris, her second cousin twice removed, who, believe me, you want to be removed from at least twice.

'*Important* things,' Opal said, hissing.

Mrs Gladstone was glaring at me like a vulture who'd just seen mouse meat. '*Ahem,*' she said pointedly.

Opal looked at Mrs Gladstone and shivered.

I sighed in defeat, released Opal's clenched hand from

my arm. 'I've got to go. We'll have lunch tomorrow. I promise.'

I walked to the Cadillac, opened the back door for Mrs Gladstone.

Starving Teen Shuns Lunch for Servitude.

'Mrs Gladstone, what is happening?'

'Take Lake Shore Drive,' she ordered, 'and then we shall see.'

Four

*I*T COULD HAVE BEEN WORSE, I SUPPOSE.

I pulled up to Mrs Gladstone's brownstone at 5:17, having made it to Evanston and back without anything too perilous happening, like premature death. I did get lost four times, forgot to click my turn signal on twice, almost got sideswiped by a library Bookmobile, in addition to being tailgated by a man in a Porsche with an advanced case of road rage who kept leaning on his horn to pass me even though I was surrounded by cars on either side. My grandmother used to say that some men *become* their cars. I almost ran out of gas because I wasn't watching the Cadillac tripometer that blinked digital displays that only a graduate from Massachusetts Institute of Technology could understand. I say almost because I was pulling into a Sunoco station just as the gas gave out and the great car sat there gasless in the middle of the street. This caused Mrs Gladstone to have a screaming fit about responsibility and how people in Texas never let the gas gauge go below empty because Texas is so big, it'll eat you up as sure as look at you. When the two attendants pushed us to the pump, I said wouldn't it have been awful if this had happened on Lake Shore Drive and she didn't say anything.

'Here we are,' I said coming to a lurching stop by her front door. 'Safe and sound. Technically.' I pressed the control button for the garage door. Up it went. I eased the behemoth car inside, pressed the button to close the garage door.

'I suppose you'll do,' she said.

'I'm sorry?'

'You may be my driver.' She said this like she was giving me a present.

'Mrs Gladstone, I need to be honest with you. I'd rather sell shoes.'

'I need a driver.'

'I understand that, but I bet there are whole communities of people in this town who could—'

Madeline Gladstone stomped her foot at the back door. I got out, opened it, helped her out of the Cadillac.

'I need a driver for the summer, young woman. Someone who can drive me down to Texas for the annual stockholders meeting where I will officially retire as president of the company and hand the reins of leadership over to my . . . son.' She said *son* quietly.

'You want me to drive you to Texas?'

'Not initially. First I want you to drive me to Peoria, Springfield, St Louis, Kansas City, Little Rock, Shreveport, and then to Texas. There are stores there that I must visit.'

'Excuse me for asking, Mrs Gladstone, but why don't you just fly?'

Her eyes narrowed. 'I'm seventy-three years old. I've been in the shoe-selling business for fifty of those years. Shoes get sold on the ground, not in the air!'

Got it.

I leaned towards her. 'You want us to go on a road trip?'

Her cheek twitched slightly.

'But why me, Mrs Gladstone? I mean, I'm not so good at this.'

She looked at me hard. 'Because you remind me of myself when I was a young girl.'

I studied her. To begin with, I was nearly a foot taller. Maybe she started out larger and shrank.

'I'm not only in need of a driver,' she explained. 'I need someone who has a rudimentary understanding of the shoe business. I've watched you at the store. You have an unusual knack for appreciating the customer's needs. I will pay you double your daily salary and commissions because the hours will be long. I will pay all travel accommodations, meals, and provide reasonable spending money. Upon our *safe* return to Chicago, you could receive an additional bonus. We will be gone for six weeks. I trust that will be satisfactory.'

Driving for Dollars. She wasn't that crazy.

'I'll have to ask my mother.'

'I would be happy to discuss any concerns your mother might have.'

'She'll have some, Mrs Gladstone.' I didn't say beginning with your sanity.

I looked at the Cadillac and tried to picture myself on the open road, driving away from everything.

Five

M Y MOTHER PUT DOWN HER FAVOURITE PARING knife, pushed aside the vidalia onions that were about to become baked sherried onion soup, and uttered a loud, immovable, 'No!'

I had just thrown out the plan.

'Absolutely not,' she continued. 'You haven't been driving long enough, honey. It takes time to become a mature driver.'

I tossed back my hair with total maturity and looked at the Rand McNally Road Atlas on the kitchen table that I had opened to Texas. My finger followed the wavy border separating Texas and Oklahoma.

'I think I'm being reasonable, Jenna. Six weeks is a long time.'

I studied the map. Dallas, Houston, San Antonio.

'Just tell her you're terribly flattered, you wish you could help, but your protective, yet enlightened mother said no.' Mom held her head like she was getting a migraine and let the window fan blow her short black curls back. 'It's not,' she added, 'that I don't trust you.'

I looked at the map and sighed.

Trusted Teen Takes Texas by Storm.

'It's the other people on the road,' Mom said. 'The maniac drivers, the idiots, the—'

'Rest-stop serial killers.'

'It's been known to happen, Jenna.'

'I've never been to Texas, Mom.' I watched her face for signs of guilt. Her black eyebrows furrowed. Not good.

'Dad's back.' I had to tell her.

The paring knife crashed on the cutting board.

'*What?*' I saw the shadow cross her face.

'He came to the store,' I added.

'Drunk?' Her voice was thick with anger.

'I've seen him worse.'

'How comforting.' Mom slapped an angry fist on the counter. 'What did he do this time?'

I threw up my hands. How do you explain it?

'*What did he do?*'

'He was yelling my name, he kept falling over, he embarrassed me in front of the world! Just the usual, Mother! *OK?*'

Mom closed her green eyes that exactly matched Faith's. 'I'm sorry, Jenna.'

'Mom, I want to get out of town. It gets so weird when Dad—'

'You don't have to see him!'

'*He's my father! What do you want me to do when he comes around? Walk away? Leave him lying in the gutter! I can't do that! I've got to know he's OK! I've got to make sure he gets some place safe! I don't hate him like you do!*'

'*That's not fair!*'

'*None of this is fair!*' I slammed the atlas shut. 'Every time Dad comes back in town we all get crazy! He makes things so hard!' I picked up the atlas, hugged it to my chest.

Mom gripped the sink, steadied herself. 'I need to think,' she said quietly.

'I do, too. Mrs Gladstone's offering me a lot of money.'

'Yes,' Mom said guardedly. 'She is.'

I kept thinking about Mrs Gladstone's job offer, mostly

with my calculator to get the full monetary impact. We were talking big bucks. Enough bucks with what I already had in the bank to buy a signficant used car in the fall.

A car.

Freedom.

But then, as Opal said when I talked to her about it, there was the amount of money I would spend on psychiatric care because Mrs Gladstone would drive me over the edge.

'Two weeks tops,' Opal warned. 'You'll be whimpering on the Interstate, pleading to come home.'

'She's not that bad.'

'She's a bonafide Hansel and Gretel-eating witch! We're talking here, Jenna, about the ultimate summer from hell!' Opal leaned closer, her blue eyes dulled by confinement. 'And I know from *hell*.'

Mom was thinking about it, too. Collecting facts, actually – that's how she thought about things. She talked to Mrs Gladstone. She talked to Murray. She took me out on the Kennedy Expressway in the Honda during rush hour and barked orders at me from the backseat. She gave me wrong directions and made me find my way home. She even pretended to have a heart attack when we were getting gas and I had to lay her out flat on the backseat and tell the woman in the Plymouth Voyager not to call 911 because my mother was a real kidder.

The phone calls started Thursday night, three AM.

Dad was at a bar – drunk, sappy. 'Now, Jenna girl, I want you to say a big hello to Sueann, the woman who's changed my life.'

Friday night, two-thirty.

'Now, Jenna girl, you got to understand that your mother makes it hard for me to come around. It's not that I don't want to.'

Saturday afternoon, 5:17.

'Now, Jenna girl, I'm coming over and we're going to have a talk like we used to and I'm going to bring a pizza and we're going to catch up'

'No, Dad.'

He didn't like that so I lied and told him I was sick and had to get some sleep and maybe we could get together when I was feeling better.

'Dad,' I said quietly, 'are you all right?'

Never better, he said, and over the receiver I heard the sound of shattering glass.

Beer bottle, he explained.

After that, I stopped answering the phone.

'Did he ask about me?' Faith kept asking.

Mom was storming around, saying how Dad would push himself on us for a month or so every few years to make up for all the years he wasn't around. She confronted him the next time he called. He asked for me; she wouldn't put me on. He blew up, saying no one gave him a chance. He's coming over to talk to his daughter!

Not when you're drunk, Mom shouted back. And, by the way, you have *two* daughters, and let's not forget you haven't sent a child support payment in months!

I came into the kitchen as she slammed down the phone. She was steeling herself like she did at the hospital when a tough case came in.

Mom, please let me go.

'I need to get out of here,' I said. 'I need to go to Texas.'

Mom leaned against the wall, studied my face.

'OK,' she said finally. 'OK.'

Six

I HAD TWO DAYS TO PACK, WHICH WAS CLOSE TO impossible since no one could tell me what to bring for six weeks on the road with a fussy rich person. There was so much to do, but packing wasn't as important as seeing my grandmother.

I walked into her room at the Shady Oaks Nursing Home. She was sitting in a green vinyl chair looking out the window at nothing in particular, holding her old sewing kit in her lap that Mom brought from her shop. One side of her hair was matted like she'd been sleeping on it. She was wearing the pink sweater I gave her two Christmases ago. She never went anywhere without that sweater.

I held out the bunch of daisies I'd brought her. She smiled at the flowers. She used to have a field of them behind her house in Wisconsin; we'd pick them fresh every day when I visited. Before she got Alzheimer's, her eyes had been a crackling blue. Now they were like looking into muddy water.

'I'm going on an adventure, Grandma. I'm driving to Texas.'

'Texas.' She said the word like it was a person she was trying to remember.

'I'm going to eat barbecue and learn the two-step and wear a cowboy hat and touch an oil rig.'

'Oh,' said Gladys, her roommate, 'I been to Texas.

Never seen such a place – sky so big, and so wide. You tell Texas hello for old Gladys.'

'I will. I'll bring you back a piece of the sky.'

Gladys laughed and jiggled the plastic blue bracelets I gave her at Christmas.

'Texas,' my grandmother said flatly, but she took my hand when she said it. I sat there with her for the longest time not saying anything. I opened the quilted top of her sewing kit that had been the beginning of so many projects. Grandma touched the antique thimbles, the threads in every colour, the fine scissors from France.

'Do you remember that rainbow skirt you made for me, Grandma? It had eight different fabrics, each a different colour. It was my favourite thing to wear.'

I took her big scrapbook out of her dresser drawer. When she knew the disease was coming, Grandma started stockpiling memories the way people collect canned goods and batteries when a bad storm is coming. She and I went through all her pictures, got them in books. She said memories were so precious, she wasn't going to let some infernal disorder take them from her. I opened the scrapbook to a photo of me at ten in the rainbow skirt, twirling in the park, the skirt flowing out, catching the wind.

I pointed to the photo. 'That's the one, Grandma. You used your sewing kit to make it. It was the best skirt in the world. All my friends were jealous.'

She studied the picture and held her sewing kit tight.

I walked to her memory board and put up a picture of myself with a sign I made that read, "Jenna's gone to Texas. She'll see you when she gets back."

'When I come back we're going to have that picnic,' I promised. I put the daisies in water and kept one out. I put it in her hand. 'I remember how we used to pick daisies, Grandma, at your house, and Faith tried to eat them once when she was small. I loved going to your house.'

She squeezed the daisy tight like it held all her memories.

'OK, Faith, you're sure you know how to take the bus up to see Grandma?'

Faith was sitting on the one corner of my bed that didn't have luggage on it. We'd been through the directions three times. She nodded. I handed her a supply of bus tokens.

'You've got to see her every week and go through her scrapbooks with her and put things up on her memory board and tell her about the times you remember.' I handed her a container of thumbtacks. Faith took them, unsure.

'I just feel so weird in that nursing home, Jenna. I never know what to say and I can't wait till I leave.'

'I know. I'll tell you my secret. I remember that Grandma can't help it. I remember how she never left us. And I tell myself that for one hour a week, I can be strong for her.'

'I'll try.'

'I know you will.' I didn't say *you'd better*, even though I was thinking it. 'And if Dad comes around, what do you do?'

Faith gulped hard. 'If I think he's drunk, I tell him I can't see him now.'

'And?'

She bit her lip. 'I tell myself he's got a disease and it doesn't have anything to do with me.'

I handed her a pamphlet: *Is someone you love an alcoholic?*

Faith took it and curled up in the patchwork quilt Grandma made me. I folded my yellow bathrobe carefully. Too much was swirling in my mind.

How would Faith and Mom manage without me?

Would Dad come around drunk?

Would Grandma be all right?

And what about Mrs Gladstone and me in that car for six whole weeks?

I wondered if I was about to make the biggest mistake of my promising young life.

Seven

'WELL,' MOM SAID, TRYING TO BE TOUGH. WE were standing at Mrs Gladstone's front door, having been through the goodbyes already. Mom cried a little at the house. Faith got hostile because I didn't have time to do the dishes. She got over it, though. We gave each other a suffocating, rib-busting Boller goodbye hug. Opal called and said I could phone her anytime day or night and she promised not to say I told you so. I rammed the lion door knocker as thunder sounded in the distance – a warning sign from God.

Maria opened the door, grinning. She was going to have the house to herself for six weeks. Mrs Gladstone stood in the hall, wearing at trench coat and a hat with a feather; she was leaning on a cane. I'd never seen her with a cane before. It was probably to whack me on the head if I did something wrong. She walked slower than usual to Mom and handed her an itinerary of our trip with phone numbers and addresses.

I put my suitcases in the hall and told Mom she should probably go. 'I'm not going to camp,' I whispered. 'I'm being paid. It's a grown-up thing.'

Mom nodded and left, her shoulders shaking. Thunder clapped as we walked to the garage.

Mrs Gladstone stood regally by the car door and rapped her cane on the floor. 'And now, young woman, how much experience have you had driving in storms?'

'Not much, ma'am.' I opened the back door for her and watched her get in; her face looked pained when she sat down. 'Unless you're talking metaphorically,' I added, 'and then I'm a total ace.'

I gripped the wheel and stared through the wipers that were whizzing full blast against the heavy rain. The Chicago wind picked up a garbage can lid and hurled it over the Cadillac. I turned left, keeping an eye out for arks, and headed towards Lake Shore Drive, *slowly*. In Driver's Ed we spent an entire period on hydroplaning (what happens when you drive too fast in the rain) – water sticks to the tyres, the tyres ride up on the water, you have no control of the car. It basically means you're doomed. I drove fifteen miles an hour in a thirty-five mph zone, which the truck driver behind me didn't appreciate. Some people have a built-in prejudice against teenage drivers.

I looked at Mrs Gladstone through the rearview mirror. She took a blue pillow out of her big purse and tried to place it under her right hip. She looked up, caught me staring.

'Eyes on the road,' she barked.

I drove – past Oak Street Beach, Navy Pier, Grant Park, Soldier Field. I stared straight ahead at the Stevenson Expressway sign, just visible through the downpour. I could hear Mrs Gladstone moving around, trying to get her leg pillow in place.

'Are you OK, Mrs Gladstone?'

'I am.'

'Did you hurt your leg?'

'This leg will make it to Texas,' she declared and rapped her cane against the door.

That was good. You hate to leave things like legs by the side of the road. I pulled onto the expressway ramp, signalling to all approaching vehicles that I was attempting to merge in a monsoon. I prayed, gripped the wheel, pushed my right foot on the accelerator, and steered the Cadillac between an old school bus and a stationwagon.

I watched the Chicago skyline move away from me, caught the last of it in the rearview mirror. I had so many plans for this summer and now everything had changed. I waved goodbye to Gladstone's and Murray and all my regulars who would have to be fitted without me. Said good riddance to the dirty grey hallways of John F. Kennedy High, my so-so performance on the basketball team, the awful memory of Dad reeling drunk in Gladstone's, the drunken late-night calls. My heart tugged at the thought of my grandmother in her green chair; my mother being brave; Faith trying to be strong; Opal needing to talk about *things*. I had a quick flash of Matt Wicks and wondered what it would have been like if he'd just noticed me once. My stomach rumbled at the loss of thick-crust Chicago pizza and Polish sausage with grilled onions.

I thought of all the places I was going where I had never been and wondered how I would manage.

But when you sell shoes, you learn first-hand about flexibility.

I embraced my motto, Cope or Die, breathed deeply, and headed for Peoria.

We made it to Peoria in southern Illinois in four hours flat due to the torrential downpour and the road construction on I 91 that kept traffic to one lane even though the construction crew had given up long ago and gone home.

I was getting pretty good at driving in the rain and so far Mrs Gladstone had slept in the back, having taken two yellow pills. She did snore, unfortunately – loud, snuffling, Texas-sized snorts. My grandma always said that people who snored were sleeping with enthusiasm. I tried to remember this, but there's just so much enthusiasm a person can handle in close quarters.

Mrs Gladstone and I had lunch in a diner overlooking the Illinois river, which was about to reach flood stage. Any moment now people would begin hurling sand bags along the banks. Mrs Gladstone pushed aside her meatloaf Wellington lunch special.

'I suppose I should call Miles and let him know we're coming.'

She was referring to Miles Wurlitzer, manager of the Gladstone's Shoe Store in Peoria.

'It's better to give employees short notice,' Mrs Gladstone said, pulling her cellular phone out of her canvas bag. 'Gives you a better sense of what's really happening at the store.'

Mrs Gladstone pressed phone buttons. 'Miles, dear, it's Madeline Gladstone. Surprise. I'm just down the road.'

I pictured the poor man slumped in horror.

Mrs Gladstone slapped her phone shut and watched the river, looking sad.

I thought about what it had to be like to be retiring from her business after all these years. My mother always said the best way to get to know someone was to walk around in their shoes. I didn't think my 9½s could squeeze into her size 6s, but I gave it a go.

'I bet this is a pretty complicated trip for you, Mrs Gladstone, with you retiring and all.'

She sucked in air and stared out the window.

'I heard when my grandfather retired from the meat department at Grossinger's, he missed it pretty bad, just spent hours opening and closing the refrigerator at home because he was so used to working in the cold slicing up all that beef.'

Nothing.

'Well, I think like anything, Mrs Gladstone, it's going

to take some getting used to, but like my grandma always said, change is good for you. It might not seem that way in the beginning, but if you stay with it, you'll see. My grandma knew about change, too, because she owned a tailor shop. She said all she needed was for people to gain weight or lose it, or for hemlines to shoot up or down – it didn't matter to her.'

I told her how Grandma had been widowed three times. How when her third husband, Lars, died, she said if I saw her heading for the altar again I'd better scream bloody murder until she turned around.

'After that she just dated,' I explained.

'Your grandmother sounds like a piece of work.'

'She was that, Mrs Gladstone. You could stick my grandma in a room full of men and in thirty minutes tops she'd find the richest one in the place.'

Mrs Gladstone made a little noise close to laughing. 'Is this a gift that runs in your family?'

'No, ma'am. We don't hang with rich people much.'

Oops. I tried to save myself.

'Not that there's anything wrong with rich people. I mean, personally, I like rich people.'

I needed to change the subject.

'And what do you like about them?'

Jeeze. My mind reached for something.

'Well, I like you, Mrs Gladstone, and let's face it, you're not hurting. I mean, you could have had any driver money could buy probably, but you decided to give me a chance and all this responsibility not to mention a good salary and . . .' I trailed off here.

Mrs Gladstone leaned forward, chuckling. 'Jenna, in Texas we say there's rich and there's Texas rich. Just so you know, I'm somewhere in between.'

Miles Wurlitzer was buzzing around the cash register with

a dust cloth and very wild eyes. He hid the cloth behind his back when Mrs Gladstone walked through the glass door.

'Mrs Gladstone,' he croaked out, 'What a wonderful surprise.'

Liar, liar, pants on fire.

Mrs Gladstone looked quickly in every corner, her grey eyes missed nothing. 'Just exactly how are things in Peoria?' she asked.

Miles wiped his moist brow with the dust cloth. 'Just great, Mrs Gladstone. Really great.'

I looked around the store, too. Only one customer. One customer on Saturday afternoon during peak shopping time after a rain storm. Not too great in my book. A thin salesman put a black pump on a woman, who made a face.

'Much too tight,' she said, taking them off. Then she gathered her shopping bags and left. I wondered why the salesman hadn't shown her something else. Any true shoe professional could see that woman was on a mission for black pumps and she wasn't going to rest until she found the right ones. You've got to stay with a customer, even if they go through ten pairs. He just shrugged and watched her go. I sniffed the air. Something about this store didn't feel right. A rich-looking older woman walked in. He sighed, shuffled to her side.

'Need some help, ma'am?'

Now, true, I wasn't looking for shoes, but this guy didn't know that. Mrs Gladstone hadn't introduced me to anyone. I, a potential customer, was getting ignored and I knew why.

I was a teenager.

'Excuse me,' I said to the salesman, 'I'd like to see these loafers in a nine and a half wide.'

'I'll be with you in a minute, miss.' He returned to the older woman.

I stood extra tall, looked down at the thin salesman, and announced, 'I believe I was here first.'

Mrs Gladstone planted her cane, watching.

Miles bit the end of the dust cloth.

The older woman smiled at me and said, 'Yes, she was here first.'

This was too much for the thin salesman who got maroon and flustered and knocked over half the Nike display which was near the back by the purses, a really dumb place, since anyone who knows anything about selling shoes knows the Nike display goes up front in any store because Nikes bring customers inside. And the purses by the Nikes weren't the nice, thick leather kind that we had in the Chicago store either. I checked the inside of one. Cowhide, the label read. I felt the grade. Not much of a cow.

The salesman scurried out with a shoe box, quickly put the loafers on my feet. I took two steps.

'They're tight,' I said, feeling the cheap heels.

'They'll break in,' he said, eyeing the older customer.

I told him no, I didn't think so, not today, put my stacked leathers back on, and studied the Nike display that Miles was putting back together like he was a game show contestant and had sixty seconds to get it right or be rolled in gunge. I picked up a pair of Nike multiple sports-trainers. 'Can I use these effectively for running?' I asked.

'Oh, yes,' he said.

'For long-distance running?'

'For any kind of running.'

'Thank you.'

I walked away, not saying that I knew that multiple sports-trainers were OK for short distances but not for long ones.

Mrs Gladstone motioned me to the door with her cane. I

walked slowly past the displays that did not show off the shoes in the best light. The work boots were right across from slippers, which you don't want together no matter how small the store is. Work and leisure have to be on opposite walls. I looked at the fake leather pumps, felt the plastic soles on the children's oxfords. I strolled out the double glass door to the parking lot.

Jenna Boller, shoe spy.

I walked to the Cadillac, feeling the moist, hot air of freedom. I stared at the double glass door of Gladstone's Shoes/Peoria Branch, stared at the Gladstone's slogan, WE'RE NOT JUST SELLING SHOES, WE'RE SELLING QUALITY.

Could have fooled me.

Finally, Mrs Gladstone limped out.

She was walking stiffly, every step seemed an effort. Her cane made clicking noises on the asphalt. I opened the back door and held it open like a palace guard.

She looked at me. 'What did you see in there?'

I bit my lip because I'd seen a lot, but I wasn't sure if I should say it.

'Jenna Boller,' she said, *what did you see?*'

I took a fat breath and told her as she got into the car. I was getting worked up right there in the parking lot and I got very heated when I came to the work boot part because I am very good at doing shoe displays and know how to bring out the character in any brand. Put them in their natural environment is my secret. Display them so they look tough. Work boots always go on brick. Then I mentioned the part about being ignored because of my age and put in a word for teenagers everywhere.

'It happens a lot, Mrs Gladstone. Our money is just as good as an adult's, sometimes we've had to work longer and harder for it. Kids deserve respect when they go into a store.'

I didn't mention the shoddy merchandise.

'And what would you do with that store?' she asked.

I thought about that. 'Well, I guess first I'd change the traffic flow, move the Nikes to the window, get the slippers in the back by the purses. It doesn't matter if purses and slippers are together, Mrs Gladstone – most customers don't head for the back of the store first. I'd get the good, fast-moving stuff up front, retrain the salespeople so they understand what the shoes can do, and if they couldn't be retrained, well . . .'

'You'd hire new ones.'

I coughed. 'Yes, I would.'

Mrs Gladstone adjusted her pillow under her thigh. 'My son hired Miles.'

Good one, Boller.

'I didn't mean anything by that, ma'am. Mr Gladstone knows a lot more about the shoe business than me.'

Mrs Gladstone grunted.

I got in the front seat, strapped on my seat belt. 'I don't know what came over me in the store, Mrs Gladstone. I've got this weird way of doing things. I guess I was being deceitful. It won't happen again.'

'It better happen again!' She cracked her cane on the back door. *'Drive!'*

Eight

I DROVE.

We were on the 474 connector heading toward 155 South, which would intersect with 55 South and take us to Springfield, Illinois, land of Abraham Lincoln.

Mrs Gladstone shifted uncomfortably in the back. 'That store makes me want to lose my lunch.' Her cane whacked the door. 'How long do you think it's going to take before our customers figure out our quality is slipping?'

'I . . . I don't know, Mrs Gladstone.'

'Not too long, I can assure you!'

Another whack.

'My son is pushing me out.'

I shifted. 'I didn't know that, ma'am.'

'Now you do.'

It didn't surprise me, though. Murray called Elden the vice president in charge of tack at Gladstone's Shoes. He said Elden didn't have a shoe person's heart. All he cared about was money, not sole.

'He's decided I'm too old and he's taking over the business.'

I looked at Mrs Gladstone in the rearview mirror. Elden might be a bum, but he was right about one thing. She was old.

'He says I should relax, enjoy life, get a condo in Florida.' She winced.

'You don't want to retire?'

'Somewhere long ago in this country it was determined that after sixty-five a person's brain is no longer capable of making business decisions. I think that is rot. I have more business ability at seventy-three than I had at sixty-three, and I resent the implication that I am over the hill and can no longer oversee the company my husband and I built from scratch.'

I was about to say 'Oh,' but didn't get the chance.

A speeding truck was tailgating me, coming up close and personal to the back fender, getting so close I could see the fire of delight in the truck driver's eyes as he blared his horn at me and inched closer, closer.

'For heaven's sake, let that bully by!' Mrs Gladstone shouted.

I swerved to the far right lane, screeched onto the shoulder as the truck rumbled by shaking the pavement.

'Stop the car!'

I did. Mrs Gladstone was quiet for a long time.

'Take off your shoe,' she said finally.

'What?'

'Hand me your shoe.'

This was distinctly weird. I took off my right shoe, handed it to her, hoping it didn't stink.

She examined the stacked heel, pulled gently at the sides, felt the cushioning inside.

'This,' she declared, 'is a well-made shoe. Not too much pull on the leather, fine stitching, good sole.'

'No plastic,' I said.

'Ah, yes, plastic.' Mrs Gladstone's ancient face got tight. 'My son is quite taken with that.'

I looked down at my bare foot. 'I've noticed.'

'Do you know what built Gladstone's Shoes, Jenna?'

I gripped the steering wheel. There were several ways to go here. Sweat. Honesty. Good old American know-how.

She raised my shoe in the air. 'An unmovable insistence on quality and fair pricing. An insistence on the finest, most shoe-educated salesforce in the business.'

I nodded, remembering my one-week training course where I had to remember everything that could possibly go wrong with a shoe fitting. I learned how many bones there were in the human foot (twenty-six) including nineteen muscles, thirty-three joints, and one hundred seven ligaments. I learned that bones of the feet make up approximately one fourth of all the bones in the body, that the feet are one of the most frequently injured parts of the body. I understood that the average individual will walk about 115,000 miles in their lifetime, which is more than four times the earth's circumference, and came to the rapid conclusion that selling well-made comfortable shoes is a noble profession, providing immeasurable benefit for people the world over. Then I got my own personal shoehorn, and after my one-year anniversary, I got a shoehorn with my initials.

'Elden has cancelled the training courses for new employees,' she said. 'He just fired two of my top store managers who refused to sell his shoddy merchandise. One of them ran the Peoria store.' Her lips went tight.

I got nervous for Murray. 'Can he do that?'

'He has done it.'

'But why?'

Mrs Gladstone was staring at my shoe like it was a dead pet. 'I don't think I want to be around to witness what Elden will do to my business.'

'Boy, Mrs Gladstone, that's pretty rough.'

'It's a sad day, Jenna, when profits and greed alone influence quality. It's an even sadder day when honour in business is close to becoming a thing of the past.'

The Cadillac purred across the highway, which is what

you expect from a 32-valve, 300-horsepower V8 engine. Mrs Gladstone was stirring around in the back, rattling papers, keeping busy to manage the hurt. She seemed to trust I'd get her to Springfield, and I would. Good, loyal Jenna. Loyal like a dog. A person you can count on. Just give her a biscuit and she'll go out of her way to help. I turned south onto 55. In an hour we'd be in Springfield.

I was getting the hang of manoeuvering this big white moose after 184 miles. There's something about holding onto a steering wheel and feeling the miles drift away from you as you push farther and farther away from what you once knew.

One of the last things Mom said to me before we left the house was that even though I'd be driving a long way from home, I wouldn't be driving away from my problems. I knew this was true the way I knew that clouds weren't made of cotton, but sometimes those white clumpy clouds hanging in a grey blue sky made me wonder if God hadn't stuck some cotton balls up there when the scientists weren't looking.

I knew one thing for sure: I was glad to be away from the mess with Dad.

I didn't miss it one bit.

I let a hot red Mustang convertible pass me, catching the licence plate as the car whizzed by: ITSORED.

I sighed.

Someday.

There was good news and bad news in Springfield, Illinois.

The good news was that we got there.

The bad news was that the hotel was overbooked with the Markoy Electronics annual sales meeting and we had to share a room.

'This,' said Mrs Gladstone to the bellman, 'is not a room, it is a closet.'

The bellman, who was old and deaf, said he was glad we liked it and hoped we had a nice stay. He tottered out, waving happily. I checked out the room. One twin bed; one rollaway bed approximately five feet in length for all five feet eleven inches of me.

Mrs Gladstone lowered herself slowly onto the real bed.

'Gee, Mrs Gladstone, it isn't so bad. You should have seen the room my mother and sister and I shared last summer in the Dells. Bugs in the mattress, seedy furniture. We're talking *Les Miserables*. But you know, we had an OK time.'

Mrs Gladstone glared at the Springfield, Illinois, Visitor's Guide: *The City Lincoln Loved*, and said absolutely nothing.

The hotel restaurant, El Pollo Loco, was packed with electronics salespeople who were discussing their products loudly while pouring margaritas from pitchers into huge glasses that were big enough to raise goldfish in. There could have been goldfish in them, actually, but I didn't think the Markoy Electronics salesforce would have noticed. I knew about margaritas because my father went through a Latin American drinking phase and made margaritas at home. He did this while singing 'La Bamba.' He'd sing the 'la la la la la la la bamba' part extra high and squeeze the lime around the glass and sprinkle on plenty of salt and pour the liquor combination into the blender. Dad was very exact when he made drinks, even when he was bombed. He always reminded me of a pharmacist, measuring just the right amount of cough syrup into the bottle. Of course, unlike a pharmacist, towards the end of the evening, Dad would be measuring his concoctions on the floor.

Mrs Gladstone chewed her jalapeños without breaking a sweat. For an old person, she has grit. Three Markoy employees began an enchilada eating contest (not a pretty sight), but she wasn't paying attention. Her eyes got far away.

'I grew up along the Guadalope River,' Mrs Gladstone said quietly, gazing out the window. 'I just lived to be in water when I was a girl, couldn't stand wearing shoes. I'd kick them off every chance I'd get and stick my feet in the water, summer and winter. And now I own one hundred and seventy-six shoe stores.' She laughed. 'The good Lord knows how my father would have split his spleen laughing at that. He was always barking at me to put on my shoes. "Madeline Jean," he'd say, "you put on your shoes of peace, girl." Daddy was a Baptist minister and turned everything into a sermon. "Those aren't just shoes you're putting on," he'd shout, "those are the sandals of *God Almighty*."'

I looked at her from the corner of my eye. Some people are hard to imagine as children.

Mrs Gladstone leaned back in the wooden chair, lost in thought. 'Daddy always said that shoes take us along life's pathways, they get all muddied up, all scratched from wear. We've got to clean them up, take care of them. He said God was like a master cobbler, stretching a piece of leather over a wooden last, fastening it down with nails, carefully stitching it together to form something special. That man had three sermons about shoes.'

'I never thought about shoes that way.'

'PKs gets their share of sermonizing.'

'PKs?'

'Preacher's kids.'

I smiled. 'He didn't know about your business?'

'He died right before Floyd and I opened the first store in Dallas. He would have baptized that whole place if he'd had the chance.'

'That would have been something, Mrs Gladstone.'

The man who won the enchilada eating contest lunged towards the bathroom door marked HOMBRES. The bill came; Mrs Gladstone got out her wallet. 'I still feel like he's with me in every store Floyd and I opened. When I was a child, I'd wonder why in the world did I have a father so all-fired fixated on shoes?' She opened her hands, grinning. 'Sure made me think about selling them a little different.'

I looked down. I always wondered why I had a father who was drunk.

I haven't figured that one out yet.

Curling up on the rollaway bed made me think about laying my father out on the living room couch when he was drunk. The couch wasn't long enough for Dad (he was six foot four), so I'd bend his knees to get him to fit. Faith never had to do it. Dad always said there was a price to pay for being the oldest. You're the one who gets practiced on. His dad would beat him to a pulp over something small while his younger brother Billy got the world handed to him on a Wedgwood plate.

Billy was never as good a salesman as Dad, though.

My best memories of my dad were when he'd take me out to study salespeople. Dad said you can learn anything by watching other people do it, and if they do it badly, you learn what not to do. The worst salesperson we ever saw sold washers and dryers. He'd sweat and slap the machines and yell that he was giving people a price so low his manager was going to hang him. One customer stormed off grumbling, 'I'll get the rope.' The best salesperson sold Singer sewing machines. She liked people, liked her product, and didn't need to push anyone into buying anything they didn't want. Dad said she knew the secret. When we got home I'd practice selling to Dad whatever we saw that day, and except when I was pitching swamp land in Florida, he always bought. Afterwards he'd celebrate what a good little salesperson I was by having a few drinks, but before the booze got hold of him, he was a real father.

Mrs Gladstone's snoring was sounding like an approaching Amtrak train rumbling into Union Station. She was tossing, kicking off her sheets.

'No!' she shouted in her sleep, then bolted up with a cry.

I turned on the light. She was shaking.

'Mrs Gladstone, you were dreaming.'

She nodded and covered her face with her hands.

'Do you want to talk about it? My mom says talking about bad dreams can make them better.'

She shook her old head.

'I know about nightmares,' I assured her.

She looked straight at me. 'Yes, I suppose you do.'

I sat down on the side of her bed. 'I used to have one where I was taking a shower and instead of water coming out, it was bourbon, which is my dad's favourite drink, and I kept trying to turn off the flow, but the bourbon was washing over me and getting in my hair and eyes and mouth. I kept trying to spit it out, but I couldn't and it tasted awful and I was so afraid I was going to get drunk. It wasn't going down the drain, either, just filling up the tub, rising higher in the room until it was over my shoulders and I was sure I was going to drown in it. I woke up screaming.'

Mrs Gladstone nodded a little. 'And did I wake up . . . screaming?'

'Kind of. Well, actually, yes.'

She looked down, rubbed her sad eyes, and looked for her glasses. I took them off the nightstand, handed them to her. She put them on fast to cover the tears that were starting.

'My son,' she began, clenching her mouth to keep control, 'has been buying up Gladstone stock to gain control of the business because he was afraid I would not go quietly.'

I didn't know much about stocks. My grandma had given Faith and me both three shares of stock in her boyfriend Earl's fire alarm company so we could learn the lessons of big business. In thirteen months we watched the stock go from $15 a share to nada and Earl go from CEO to the unemployment line, so the stock market didn't hold much magic for me.

'I'm sorry, Mrs Gladstone – I don't understand.'

She grabbed a pad and pencil by the bedside table. 'You understand what a share of stock is?'

'It's like buying a tiny fraction of a company.'

'That's right. A share of stock is like a deed to a small piece of a company. Now in the case of Gladstone's Shoes, there are four million public shares available, out of a possible twelve million. Those who own the most shares, own the most of the company. The problem arises when an individual or group of investors decide they want more say in a company.'

'So they start buying more stock to get control.'

'Precisely.'

'And they can do that?'

'They can.'

'You mean anyone could take over any company they wanted if they had enough money?' I shuddered.

'Theoretically. The system has many checks and balances built in to safeguard certain practices, but companies are taken over regularly.'

'But what if the owners don't want to give them up?'

'Well, that's the rub. It doesn't much matter.'

'But that's not fair! That's like stealing!'

'Yes, it is. Elden and Ken Woldman, the president of

the Shoe Warehouse, are buying up Gladstone stock to gain control.'

The Shoe Warehouse was a big chain of budget-priced shoe stores. 'But the Shoe Warehouse can't own Gladstone's! They'd change it!'

'That seems to be their plan,' she said heavily.

I put my hand on Mrs Gladstone's bony shoulder. She tensed. I decided not to say that Elden was an all-time stinking shoe louse. I didn't know what to say, so I just sat next to her like I did with my grandmother, letting her know I was there.

'Quality first, I always told him.' Mrs Gladstone said this softly, shifting the weight from her bad hip. 'From the time he was a little boy, I would say, "Elden, there is no substitute for quality in business. When you cut corners, you lose, the customer loses. Offer the best quality and services at the best price and the result will be profits."' She stabbed her finger in the air, holding back tears. 'That is what Gladstone's has been built on. I keep hoping he'll see the light.' She shook her old head. 'I keep telling myself this isn't happening.'

She shifted her hip and looked out the window. For a minute she seemed like my grandmother. I understood about being rejected by someone you love – the carelessness of it, the pain. Elden was careless, so was my dad. You want so much to believe they'll change and love you like you need them to. You'll lie to yourself about them, make them more than they are.

'Mrs Gladstone, there's got to be something you can do.'

'It's a young person's game now.'

'You're giving up?'

She looked down. 'I'm moving aside.'

'But what about quality, what about the Gladstone name?'

'Floyd took care of those things, Jenna. I kept the books, oversaw the store expansion . . .'

I put my face close to hers so she had to look at me. 'Mrs Gladstone, I can't believe you're not going to do anything.'

Her grey eyes burned with hurt and anger. She lay back down, covered herself with a blanket, and that was that.

Nine

WE PASSED ON EL POLLO LOCO FOR BREAKFAST and hit the Honest Abe Pancake House down the street that had a tin of real maple syrup at every table and paintings depicting Abraham Lincoln's life of truth on the walls. A waitress was pouring Mrs Butterworth's syrup into a real maple syrup tin, which would have made Honest Abe split a gut.

Deception was everywhere.

Mrs Gladstone had coffee, poached eggs, and dry wheat toast. I had the Presidential platter of pigs in a blanket with a large orange juice to keep up my strength. Mrs Gladstone looked like warmed-over oatmeal and she wasn't talking much either, which is always weird when you've connected with a person one day and the next day they want to take it all back. My dad used to tell me about his big dreams to go into business for himself, even showed me the business plan he'd written once. But by the next day, he'd given up the whole thing, he didn't want to talk about it.

Inconsistency is a royal pain, but I've learned to live with it.

Mrs Gladstone and I headed towards the car in silence. Finally she said, 'I'll be having several meetings with the Springfield staff these next two days. Margaret Lundstrom, the manager, is an old friend.'

'What do you want me to do?'

'There is a Shoe Warehouse store a few blocks away. Perhaps you could use your unique talents there.'

'You want me to snoop around?'

'I didn't say that.'

I smiled, got her in the backseat, pulled the Cadillac onto the street, turned left by a statue of Abraham Lincoln that was covered with pigeons. 'You want me to be a shoe spy, Mrs Gladstone?'

'I want you to tell me everything you see, hear, and feel from the moment you walk into that store. Left here.'

'Got it.' I signalled left. 'Anything you're looking for in particular?'

'I'm looking for your insight, Jenna. Turn here.'

I did, nice and easy, the Cadillac turned perfectly under my steely control. I pulled in front of Gladstone's Shoes, Springfield, Illinois. The windows were sparkling, the sale signs promised bargains. The Nike display was up front.

'Nice store,' I said, helping Mrs Gladstone out.

'Margaret knows how to keep a store.'

She handed me a piece of paper that had the Shoe Warehouse's address. 'Come back in three hours, and for heaven's sake, don't be obvious.' She leaned heavily on her cane, walked to the glass-etched G on the door, pushed it open, and limped inside.

It's tricky not being obvious when you're a five-foot-eleven-inch female. Whenever I walk in anywhere, people usually strain their necks to look up at me. I'd trade four inches of height for beauty any day, but no one would swap. I threw back my shoulders and stood extra tall like my grandma taught me. Grandma always said there is nothing more commanding than a tall woman who uses her height. Grandma was six feet even and wore three-inch heels to make the point. I walked into the Shoe Warehouse like I owned the place.

I was glad I didn't.

First off, it was built like a factory with storage bins and steel shelving to make you think you were getting rock-bottom prices. There were sale signs and twenty-per cent-off signs and a big bell that went *bong* whenever someone bought over four pairs of shoes at once. There was green astro turf on the floor and big mirrors on the wall. The merchandise was second-rate.

I ran my finger over a large yellow display cube (dusty). A small round man wearing a green 'Shoe Warehouse' shirt sat behind the cash register drinking noisily from a can of Dr Pepper. I walked on past the low-end children's section thinking my spy thoughts.

No continuity among styles.

Bad displays.

Shoes not fully lined.

I stopped to watch an exhausted woman with five children – all five of them were trying on shoes. The woman tied red sneakers on her little daughter.

'Mommy, they hurt.'

'They're on sale, baby.' The mother felt the girl's shoes. The small, round man walked by. 'Could you help me?' she asked. 'She says they hurt.'

The man sighed like she was asking to borrow money, got on one knee, felt the girl's shoes. 'They just need to break in,' he said.

'But they hurt!'

'New shoes are supposed to hurt,' the man said and walked away.

Lies.

Manipulation.

Child abuse.

I grabbed a foot sizer and walked up to the woman. 'I can help you, ma'am.' I knelt down in front of the little girl. 'What's your name?'

'Belinda.'

'Let's see if we can find you some shoes that don't hurt, Belinda.'

I measured her feet – made sure she stood straight, positioned her foot flat on the sizer – quick scanned the children's shoe displays. Not much. 'What are you going to do in the shoes?' I asked. 'Do you need them for all-around or something specific?'

'I'm going to run and jump,' Belinda said.

'Running and jumping.'

I found two size 4s in a decent sneaker with passable padding. I put them on her, laced them up. She bounded around the store. 'These are good!'

I fitted her older son with high tops, which wasn't easy, got her two teenage daughters out of spiked heels when I showed them that they were both developing hammer toe – a condition that causes the little toe to become curled up and sore from too-tight shoes – got them both into a lower cushioning heel, and found Rodney, age eight, a decent super-human, all-black laser-zooming sneaker at twenty per cent off that wouldn't give him shin splints on the basketball court if he double-laced them tight over the ankle like I showed him.

I taught the mother how to check the shoe's fit. 'You want some room between the big toe and the tip, but not too much. See?'

The mother checked all her children's shoes herself. She shook my hand. 'I've never had anyone help me in here. You must be new.'

'I . . . don't exactly work here.'

She looked at me strangely.

'I just like to help.'

'You sure did that. Thank you.' She took out a twenty-per-cent-off coupon, gathered her brood, and headed for the cash register. I put the shoes that didn't fit back in the boxes, put the boxes back on the shelves.

'You trying to rip me off?'

It was the mother, shouting at the small round Shoe Warehouse man who was now behind the counter.

'You saying my coupon's no good?'

The man didn't look up. 'Only two pairs of shoes per coupon,' he said flatly, turning the pages of a car magazine.

I walked to the woman's side, looked at the coupon: 'Twenty per cent off – the Shoe Warehouse.'

'It doesn't say anything about a two-pair limit,' I said to the man.

'It was a misprint,' he said, still reading.

I glared at the small round man who had guilty eyes. 'Is that an official store policy?'

'Yeah.'

'Do you have it in writing?'

He shrugged.

I said, 'If you don't have it in writing, sir, you have to honour this coupon.'

'I don't have to do nothing,' the man said.

The woman was shaking, looking in her wallet. 'But I can't get all my kids shoes without that twenty per cent,' she said.

'Store policy,' said the man.

My insides were steaming. I looked out the window. A large policeman walked by twirling his nightstick. 'Stay there,' I said to the woman and ran out the door.

'Officer, we need some help.'

He put his hand on his gun – a nice touch – and stormed inside. The Law.

I showed him the coupon as the round man grew pale.

The officer walked toward him.

'Made a mistake,' the small man said, reaching for the coupon. 'It's good. We'll take it. *Sure.*'

The policeman waited until the woman paid for and got her merchandise; he held the door for her as she walked out buried in shoe boxes and children. He held the door for me, then went back in the store, said something to the small round man who nodded wildly. The policeman walked out the door whistling, tipped his hat to us, and walked off.

Another evil retail plot foiled.

The woman looked at me over her packages. 'Who are you, anyway, miss?'

I smiled mysteriously. I wished I was wearing one of those trench coats with the big collars that stand up around the neck. I put on my extra-cool driver sunglasses, touched my forehead in a tough-guy salute, and walked down the street whistling, just missing a mound of dog poop.

We stayed in Springfield for three days. I mostly poked around, took stealth walks, and wrote postcards home.

I sent Faith a completely black postcard with the words "Springfield at night," which should give her a real yuck. I got Mom a postcard of Abraham Lincoln looking presidential and wrote "Thinking great thoughts. Keeping two-and-a-half car lengths on all major thoroughfares. How's by you?" I mailed Grandma a postcard of a field of daisies and told her to pin it on her memory board. I found a card for Opal with an old-fashioned jail and wrote, "Counting the days till you'll be free."

Mrs Gladstone said I could call home whenever I wanted, but I'm not much of a phone person. I think it's because my dad used to make me answer the phone when I was small, tell people he wasn't home when he was standing right there. I didn't know at the time that he owed those people money. Dad owed more money than he could ever pay back. I don't use a phone unless I absolutely have to.

I liked being on my own. Springfield is a good town to do that in because it's easy to get around and there's so much history to see. I visited Lincoln's Tomb twice, stood there on the perfect green grass and thought about all the greatness and courage of that man. I touched the white-grey wall, wondering if some of it could rub off on me.

I love travelling and meeting new people. I met a retired couple from Canada who said that talking to me made them feel good about American teenagers. I said talking to them made me feel good about Canada, although I'd never had a reason not to. New people just take you how you come. They don't know about all the free-throws you missed in the regional basketball tournament, don't know how you looked seventeen and a half pounds thinner.

I unwrapped an Almond Joy and told Mrs Gladstone what I'd seen at the Shoe Warehouse. She said my "insights" were illuminating and wrote down everything I said in her blue leather book.

She was writing down other insights as well, mostly about Elden, heard mostly from Margaret Lundstrom, who had learned big and terrible things from Harry Bender, the world's greatest shoe salesman and manager of Gladstone's flagship store in Dallas, Texas, that was famous for its immense size (everything is bigger in Texas) and the fact that it contained the world's largest plastic foot. Harry Bender found out that Elden, the rat, was ready to sell Gladstone's to the Shoe Warehouse the day after Mrs Gladstone retired; all the meetings had taken place, the board of directors had okayed the deal without letting Mrs Gladstone know. The Shoe Warehouse wanted to use the Gladstone's name in all their tacky prefab stores so that people would think they were better than they were.

Mrs Gladstone kept talking on her portable phone to Harry Bender about it all the way back to the hotel, saying, 'Harry Bender, are you *sure?*' There'd be a pause and she'd say, '*Well!* You'd think blood would count for something.'

I didn't think customers were that dumb and I said this to Mrs Gladstone after she hung up.

'It's called perception,' she answered softly. 'Gladstone's has built such good will over the years. People trust us to sell quality merchandise. It's going to take the public a little while to catch on that just because there's a Gladstone's sign on the door doesn't mean there's Gladstone's quality inside. By then the Shoe Warehouse and Elden will be rich.'

I mentioned that it didn't seem like the Peoria store was making money with all that junky merchandise.

'That was Elden's early experiment,' she said. 'He's gotten smarter since then.'

We got to the hotel; I let the attendant park the car. Mrs Gladstone was really dragging that bad leg of hers. I could see by her face that she'd about reached her limit. I tried to mention this to her gently, but coming at her that way just got her frosted.

'I need a new hip if you must know!'

A new one? I thought you had to stay with the original.

'I'm having the operation when I return to Chicago, and I don't want to discuss it again.'

'Does it hurt bad?'

Mrs Gladstone leaned on her cane and looked at me, trying to be tough. 'This leg will make it to Texas.'

'That doesn't mean it doesn't hurt,' I said and helped her into the lobby.

Mrs Gladstone and I were turning in for the night. I was wondering how to add a foot to the rollaway bed so I wouldn't have to scrunch up like a contortionist to get some rest. I was trying to put the pillow as high up on the cot as possible to gain inches in leg room.

'Harry Bender . . .' she said. 'That man is one of a kind.'

I fiddled with the pillow, quick lay down to see if it helped. The pillow fell off. I said, 'I've heard.'

Mostly I'd heard about Harry Bender from Murray Castlebaum, who said that Harry could sell sandals to Eskimos if he felt like it. The man was a shoe legend. He sold more shoes each year than the number two, three, four, and five ranking salespeople combined.

'The great Mahatma,' Murray called him. Mahatma is a title of respect that people called Gandhi, the spiritual leader of India. It means Great Soul if you're in India. If you're in the shoe business, it means Great *Sole*.

'Mahatma Bender,' Murray would say, putting his hands together and bowing down, 'once he got them in the store, he wouldn't let them out without a sale. The man was like a magnet. People couldn't say no. If you ever meet him, all you gotta do is stand there in his presence. Believe me, kid, you'll learn something.'

Mrs Gladstone's shoulders dropped like the wind got knocked out of her.

'Is everything OK, Mrs Gladstone?'

Mrs Gladstone looked small and wrinkled propped up like she was in the bed. 'No,' she said softly. 'No, it's not.'

My mind raced back to when I was seven years old. Mom was in the kitchen pouring bourbon down the sink so there wouldn't be any for Dad to drink when he came home – if he came home. Whenever he left, even if it was just to buy cigarettes down the street, I always wondered if I'd see him again.

But this night was worse than the others. I was getting peanut butter from the pantry when Dad staggered home loaded. Mom called him an alcoholic; said he needed to get help. I'd never heard him get so angry, shouting that no one had faith in him; what's the big deal about a few drinks; couldn't a man unwind after a long day at work? He kept yelling and Mom kept saying she wasn't going to be a co-dependent anymore, wasn't going to cover up for him. He kicked a big dent in the refrigerator and stormed out.

I went out to Mom. She was crying on the kitchen stool, bent over.

'Is everything OK?' I asked her.

'No,' she said. 'No, it's not.'

From that day on I knew Dad would go permanently.

When Mom and Dad got divorced, Mom gathered me and Faith on her lap. 'We're not going to pretend like this hasn't been hard,' she said, 'because it's been very hard. We're not going to pretend that everything's OK, because right now it's not. What we're going to do is talk to each other and let our feelings out and trust that in the process we will find a better life. Deal?'

Faith said, 'Deal,' and held out her hand. She was smiling.

I said, 'Deal,' and held out my hand. I was crying.

Mom took both our hands and put them between hers. I felt strength zooming from her hands into mine, right up to my heart.

I thought about taking Mrs Gladstone's hand, but she turned off the light before I got a chance. This is what Faith does when she doesn't want to talk anymore. You could be bursting with questions and Faith yanks the light chain and leaves you sitting there in darkness, real and otherwise. Lately, with Faith, I've been yanking the light back on and glaring at her, but that sure wouldn't work tonight.

I tucked my knees up in a way that wouldn't permanently cripple my back and said, 'Sleep tight, Mrs Gladstone. Tomorrow is another day.' My grandmother used to say that to me and Faith when she tucked us in bed. It always made me hopeful.

Mrs Gladstone snorted through her ancient nose. 'Thank you, Jenna,' she said softly. 'I appreciate that.'

I waited for her heavy breathing which meant she was asleep, but it didn't come.

Ten

WHEN I WOKE UP THE NEXT MORNING, MRS Gladstone couldn't get out of bed.

'This blasted leg,' she said, struggling against the pain.

I tried to help her up, but she cried out. It hurt too much.

'I'm going to get a doctor, ma'am.'

'No, you're not.' She tried to get up again and flopped back down.

'Mrs Gladstone, you need medical help and I'm going to get it for you.'

I threw on jeans, Reeboks, my yellow Barcelona T-shirt, and ran out the door.

The elevator took forever to come. When it got to my floor it was packed with bleary-eyed Markoy Electronics people who looked like they'd spent the night hanging upside down in a meat locker. I jammed in anyway, rode to the lobby, found Chuck, the assistant hotel manager, who made a few calls and finally found an orthopedist who would come to the hotel. I went back up to the room to tell Mrs Gladstone the doctor was coming.

She wasn't happy to see me.

'You defied me,' she said.

'Yes, ma'am, I did.'

I looked down. I had practice defying adults. My father was always telling me he was fine when he was drunk, always telling me he didn't need my help when the plain truth was he needed my help sometimes to just sit down. Some adults don't always know how to take care of themselves.

She lay there looking old and miserable.

'Both Harry and Margaret feel I should attempt to stop the sale to the Shoe Warehouse,' she said quietly.

'Can you do that?'

'I don't know. Harry Bender has begun to call investors and other store managers to get their feedback.'

Mrs Gladstone pulled at the lace fringe of her night-gown and shivered in the warm room. She didn't look like she could stop a paper aeroplane.

'I want you to call the doctor and tell him to not come,' she ordered.

I took a big breath. 'Mrs Gladstone, you can keep being the tough person you are and still have a bad hip and need some help.'

She looked away.

'Because if you don't get some help it's going to eventually affect your strength, and something tells me if you and Mr Bender are going to try to save this company, you're going to need all the strength you can get, and I'm not just talking legs here.'

She sniffed.

'I don't know beans about saving companies, but I know how it works in families, and believe me, you've got to pull everybody you trust together in one place and talk real clear and plain and let everyone else do the same because there's power in truth. See, for too long at my house we just let Dad's drinking go by without anyone saying anything much about it, calling it a little problem, things like that. You've got to call a thing by its full name and that's what lets the truth out where it can get some fresh air.'

Mrs Gladstone studied my face. 'You have learned a great deal in your sixteen years.'

'Not really.'

There was a knock on the door.

She folded her arms tight. 'I don't want to see a doctor.'

I walked to the door. 'I know you don't. But you've got to.'

'And what gives you the right to order me around?'

I took a deep breath, fished around in my pocket. 'I have the car keys, ma'am.' I held them up. 'No disrespect intended.'

Mrs Gladstone grunted.

I looked through the peephole at the doctor standing in the hall, opened the door, and let her in.

Dr MacMillan wasn't taking any of Mrs Gladstone's guff, which I was glad to see. It gets lonely being the only reasonable person in the room. She told Mrs Gladstone her hip was in bad shape and got to hear her speech about how that leg was going to make it to Texas. Dr MacMillan said she needed to get X-rays, which made her split an atom, especially when the two ambulance men came to carry her off to the hospital, and she declared she wasn't going to be 'hoisted from bed by strangers' and rapped one of the attendants on the shoulder with her cane.

'*Jenna* will help me,' she declared.

'Is she always like this?' the attendant asked, rubbing his shoulder.

'Pretty much.'

I leaned over the bed so Mrs Gladstone could put her arms around my neck and I could lift her up. This seemed dumb with two strong men in the room who did these things regularly. Of course, I was taller than both of them.

Pain flashed across her face, but I got her up. And eventually, after a few false starts, into the ambulance where she would not lie down on the cot. She sat there staring straight ahead, bony arms crossed tightly against her chest, informing the attendant she did not need her blood pressure checked, the problem was her *hip*.

I said, 'They're going to take it eventually, Mrs Gladstone. Here or at the hospital. My mom's a nurse and you can't come in with a broken nail and get out without someone checking your blood pressure.'

I looked at her face, how hard and determined it was. I thought about what she and her husand had to do to build their company from the ground floor up, store by store, all 176 of them, for all those years. Women weren't in business much back then. I bet she knocked their socks off.

I took a real chance with my future, leaned close to her ear and said, 'Save it, Mrs Gladstone, for the real fight. You know?'

She sniffed hard. Then gradually her face relaxed. She nodded slightly.

'Well, for mercy's sweet sake,' she barked at the attendant. 'Are you going to take my blood pressure or not?'

Eleven

DR MACMILLAN HAD MRS GLADSTONE STAY overnight in the hospital for observation and told her what she already knew. She needed a new hip.

'Sooner rather than later,' the doctor said.

'I am scheduled for an operation in September.'

'I wouldn't recommend waiting that long,' said the doctor, writing out a prescription and suggesting she not take stairs.

Then she said it wouldn't be a bad idea to have a wheelchair in the car just in case, and Mrs Gladstone said a wheelchair was out of the question. The doctor handed me a pad with scrawled instructions that looked like hieroglyphics on what kind of wheelchair to buy. 'Just in case I'm right,' she whispered.

I packed up our suitcases, checked us out of the hotel, got the car, and asked Mrs Gladstone if we should take a run over to the medical supply store to look at wheelchairs. This went over like a pop chemistry quiz the day before spring vacation when you had to wonder for a whole week if you'd destroyed your grade point average.

'*You are to keep those infernal things away from me, do you hear?*'

'Just trying to cover all the bases, Mrs Gladstone. I know it's the last thing you want. I'm worried about you is all and—'

'Don't be.'

This whole trip was beginning to be a whole lot more than I'd bargained for.

'Mrs Gladstone, I'm not a nurse and if anything happened that I couldn't handle—'

'If I need a nurse, I'll hire one. Now I suggest, young woman, that you do what I've hired you to do.'

I gave the Cadillac extra gas to let her know I was mad.

We were heading to 55 South which would take us to St Louis, the Gateway to the West. From school, I remembered that the explorers Lewis and Clark started their expedition in St Louis. From Dad, I knew about the city's number-one product, Budweiser beer.

Mrs Gladstone had me turn on a radio station that played the big band music of World War II, which, trust me, you either like or you don't. My grandmother would have liked it, but for a sophisticated teenager it was like Chinese water torture. I focused on something else to avoid screaming – eavesdropped actually, as Mrs Gladstone talked to Harry Bender on the phone again, saying that she didn't see what could be done and wasn't it too late to win back the company? An old school bus painted baby blue from the Anointed Saints of the Evangelical Free Gospel Church of Jesus Christ, Vernon, Illinois, screeched in front of me. I rammed on the brakes to avoid hitting the back of the bus with the sign that said HEAVEN IS OUR REAL HOME.

'Mercy,' said Mrs Gladstone, jolting forward.

'I'm sorry.'

I slowed down, keeping two bus lengths between me and heaven, and pulled onto 55 South. I focused on the road; I had to be sharp. This always energized me. I didn't think too much, just clicked into the driving rhythm as the rows of highway lights curved over the pavement. I drove slowly around a blinking warning sign set up around a construction site; checked my mirrors for approaching cars when I saw a merge arrow; moved to the right lane when the driver behind me flashed his headlights. It seemed to me that the people who made the rules of the road had figured out everything that would help a person drive safely right down to having a sign that tells you you're passing through a place where deer cross. Somebody should stick up some signs on the highway of life.

CAUTION: JERKS CROSSING.

Blinking yellow lights when you're about to do something stupid.

Stop signs in front of people who could hurt you.

Green lights shining when you're doing the right thing.

It would make the whole experience easier.

Life was too hard sometimes. I let out a lonely sigh and realized how much I missed my mother.

I missed Chicago, too. And Opal.

I even missed Faith.

I missed being with people under seventy years of age.

I missed selling shoes and listening to real music.

I missed tacos and refried beans and all-night Chinese take-out places and buses and teenage conversation.

I missed my grandmother and the fun we used to have. The loss of that was like a giant crater in my heart.

I wondered how she was getting along; wondered if she remembered enough to miss me.

What if Grandma slipped too far away while I was gone?

What if Murray hired someone who could sell shoes even better than me?

What if Dad bothered Faith?

What if he never came back?

I started crying – never appropriate for a professional driver. I looked for the next place to pull off because the pain of my grandmother and my father and my homesickness and my worry were bursting out at the same time.

Tears rolled down my cheeks. I hoped Mrs Gladstone was looking out the window because I didn't think she'd appreciate this behaviour. I steered off the exit ramp, not asking permission. Mrs Gladstone didn't say anything, she just let me pull into the parking lot of Pru's Pie Palace, and run inside.

I stood by the sink in the bathroom and washed my face with cold water to get the red splotches off from all the crying and despair. No paper towels. I stuck my face under the hand blower which made my eyes tear, praying no one would walk in. If Opal was here she would have told me that tears weren't anything to be ashamed of, that crying in front of people just makes you closer. That's how Opal and I met. She was crying at the bus stop after school. Her new wallet had been stolen and she didn't have enough money to get home. I paid her fare and we rode home together. By the time we'd passed North Avenue, I'd told her my dad was an alcoholic, she'd told me her aunt believed in alien abduction, and we'd become best friends right there on the 22 North. Like my grandma always said, you never know the blessings that can come from suffering.

I dried my eyes on my sleeve and walked out to where Mrs Gladstone was sipping coffee. There were two pieces of coconut cream pie on the table, my absolute favourite dessert. I sat down reverently in front of all those calories.

She leaned forward, studying me. 'You want to talk about it?'

I shook my head. I figured she'd make me spill my guts, but she didn't.

'Some things go too deep for words,' is all she said.

And we sat there eating our pie.

Twelve

W E MADE IT TO ST LOUIS BY NIGHTFALL – DROVE
past the Gateway Arch on the Mississippi riverfront
with all those city lights gleaming like stars. The arch
represented the gateway to the west where the pioneers
began their journey to the new land. Mrs Gladstone said it
was 630 feet high. Seeing it made me feel like I'd just done
something important. I thought of all those pioneer
teenagers pushing westward in the covered wagons – hot,
sweaty, wondering what the new land would bring, trying
to convince their parents to let them drive.

I was getting very good at finding hotels. I came to a
perfect stop with no lurching in front of the St Louis
Beauregard and really impressed the doorman, who was
dressed like the Nutcracker from the ballet, except he
wasn't wearing tights. He helped Mrs Gladstone out as a
teenage boy drove by; his father was screaming instructions at him from the passenger seat: *Slow down!
Watch the light! Brake!* I smiled maturely. Those days
were over for me.

Mrs Gladstone and I checked in (separate rooms) and
headed upstairs. She was limping bad and said she was
going to have dinner in her room and that I should do the
same.

Room service.

Freedom.

I went to my room – it had a huge TV and a queen-size

bed with a painting over it that looked like the artist put ink in his mouth and spat it back on the canvas. I flopped on the bed and felt at least nineteen. It would have been great to have Opal here. She's the first friend I've ever had who I could tell everything to. With the others, I always held back about Dad and our problems, afraid that if people knew how weird things were, they wouldn't like me. With Opal, the more I tell her, the closer we get.

I looked at the room service menu: steak, lamb chops, pork medallions, turkey club, chocolate mousse cake. My stomach growled. Opal and I could make fast work of that menu. We once ate two large double cheese pizzas in one night with a six-pack of Mountain Dew and two quarts of toffee almond ice cream.

Bingeing alone is not as meaningful.

The phone rang. I waited three rings, picked it up.

'*Young woman!*'

'Yes, ma'am.'

'I need your help after all.'

So much for freedom.

I hung up and headed down the hall to Mrs Gladstone's room, knocked on the door. After a long time, she opened it. She looked pale and shaken. I walked in. She pointed to a note on the bed.

'Apparently Elden will be joining us tomorrow,' she said heavily.

'You mean here?'

'He has a business opportunity he must discuss with me immediately.'

'What kind of opportunity?'

'The message didn't say. I need you to get in touch with Harry Bender.'

'Me?'

She sighed. 'You. I have already taken my pain medication. It's making me very groggy.' Her old eyes looked cloudy. 'Tell him that Elden is coming to St Louis. Write down everything Harry says and we'll talk in the morning.' Mrs Gladstone moved slowly to the bed. 'I need to lie down.'

'Well, shoot, how's the old girl doing?'

I was sitting on my queen-size bed with the phone tucked under my chin and a legal pad in my lap, having just told Harry Bender that Elden was coming to St Louis and Mrs Gladstone asked me to call.

'Not too great, Mr Bender.'

'Blast, that's a shame. That spurless son of hers isn't going to make the situation any sweeter.'

I wrote down 'spurless son – not sweeter.'

'Here's what you got to do,' said Harry Bender in a booming Texas voice, ''cause Maddy's got to be in bad shape if she's not calling herself. You've got to diffuse the situation because that boy's coming to town with bad news for sure.'

I wrote down 'diffuse situation – bad news for sure' and said, 'Me?'

'That's right.'

'How do I do that?'

'You tell him Maddy's hurting too bad to see anyone and you'll take the message.'

'But he's not going to tell me anything.'

'That's right. And in this situation, ignorance is golden.'

I wrote down 'ignorance is golden' and waited.

''Cause, you see, old Elden's trying to slink between two camps. You can't trust what he's going to say and Maddy needs to be surrounded by the truth before the lies start breaking in around her.'

'What if I goof up?'

'You're not going to do that,' Harry Bender insisted. 'You're going to reject that thought. You're going to tell yourself you've got more than enough on the ball to pull this off. All you've got to do, no matter what old Elden says, is to smile and tell him that you absolutely understand, but his mother can't see anyone today.'

'But what if he gets mad at me?'

Harry Bender laughed. 'You just remember, never go punching a man who's chewing tobacco.'

'Well . . .'

'Don't think it to death. Just approach him nice and friendly. You got any questions, call old Harry. Nighty night.'

Click.

I wrote 'never punch a man who's chewing tobacco.'

I think at the very least this should be a bumper sticker, but I'm not sure what any of this has to do with selling shoes.

The next morning I told Mrs Gladstone everything Harry Bender said right down to the never punch a man who's chewing tobacco part, which made her laugh out loud, even though she was hurting.

I was sitting at a table by the front of the Fichus Tree Restaurant, telling myself I had more than enough on the ball to pull this off, looking for Elden Gladstone. He was fifteen minutes late, which made me mad because for all he knew he was keeping his own mother waiting even though she was upstairs and I was her designated eater. The Fichus Tree had one of those breakfast buffets that's so loaded with food it almost makes you forget how many people go to bed hungry. I was wearing my khaki suit that made me look older and my stacked leather shoes. Shoes are an important statement when you're meeting another shoe person, since shoe people always look at someone from the ground up.

There was a jerk of movement and Elden Gladstone

sped off the elevator, pushing through the lobby like he owned it, talking angrily on a cell phone. He gave the hostess a sneer.

'I'm meeting my mother.' He looked impatiently at the tables. Seeing him made me feel tired. 'Because I *can't*,' he barked into the phone. 'It's not going to fly!'

I stood up. 'Uh, Mr Gladstone. Your mother asked me to meet you.'

He said, 'Later,' into the phone and snapped it shut. He looked at my shoes.

'I'm Jenna Boller, her . . . assistant.' Assistant sounded better than driver.

Elden reached for a handful of butter mints by the cash register and ate them all at once. He was wearing a beige floppy suit with the sleeves pushed up and a gold watch.

I steeled myself.

Smiled nice and friendly. 'She's not feeling too well, sir. She won't be coming down for breakfast.'

He glared at me, unsure. 'What's the matter with her?'

'Her hip.'

'Again?'

I didn't know this was an on-going problem. I nodded.

I took a deep breath for the next part. 'She said you could give me any message and—'

'I don't think so.'

I didn't either.

'I don't know who you are, *miss*, but I'd like to see my mother.'

'I appreciate that, sir. She just can't see anyone today. I understand how you feel.'

Elden was six inches shorter than me and he didn't like it. 'Sit down,' he barked.

I sat. He kept standing, telling me that he'd flown in from Dallas to see his mother and he wasn't leaving until that happened. I smiled, explained again and again.

'It's such a shame,' I said. 'You coming all this way. She just can't see anyone today.'

He looked at me like I was garbage. 'I'm not going to let some overgrown *teenager* tell me I can't see my mother.'

Smile.

Never kill in public.

I wanted to so bad. I looked at Elden, who was gunning for a showdown, waiting for me to lose it right there. Never punch a man who's chewing tobacco, that's what Harry Bender said. I knew why now. They spit it out all over you. I killed him with kindness.

'Boy, I'm sure sorry about this, sir. Your mother's just not able to—'

'That's clear!' Elden turned on his tasseled Italian loafer. 'You tell my mother we've got to talk. No, tell her we're *going* to talk.'

I smiled. 'I'll tell her, sir.' I felt that adding 'you ungrateful slimeball' would have been pushing it.

And with that Elden Gladstone stomped off in a stinking cloud of deceit.

Evil Retreats in the Presence of Goodness.

What a snake.

Thirteen

I GRABBED A QUICK SIP OF MY EXTRA-THICK COFFEE milk shake and said into the phone, 'Mr Bender, I'm from Chicago. I'm not sure what you mean about not drinking downstream from the herd.'

I could hear Harry Bender clear his throat. I'd just told him how things had gone with Elden. Mrs Gladstone had asked me to pass it along.

'Oh, wait a minute.' I pictured horses relieving themselves in a pure mountain stream. I made a face. 'I get it.'

'You're catching on,' Harry Bender said. 'Got to find us a safe place in this situation. In AA we say, "God grant me the serenity to accept the things I cannot change, the courage to change the things I can, and the wisdom to know the difference."'

AA stands for Alcoholics Anonymous, an important organization that helps people stop drinking. 'You're in AA?'

'Twenty-three years.'

'Wow. I really respect that, sir.' We got my dad to go to one meeting. He stormed home saying he didn't need to be sitting around with all those losers.

'Saved my bacon, I'll tell you. I was flat out in the gutter slurping slop. You tell Maddy I'm finding support for her out in the field. Lots of stockholders want the company to stay like it is, but Elden's talking big money and people like that kind of talk.'

'Is she going to lose the company, sir?'

'Not while I'm breathing.'

I smiled. 'I'm looking forward to meeting you, Mr Bender.'

'We'll have us a high old time. See you in Texas.'

Mrs Gladstone had her meetings in her hotel room over the next few days so she could stay in bed and nurse her bad hip. She insisted on getting completely dressed, right down to matching shoes, and then laid back down in bed. I mentioned that her hip seemed to be doing worse and she nearly bit my head off. She wouldn't let anyone feel sorry for her and the minute anyone did, she'd just wave it off like no one had the right to care. She got away with this with me and three store managers.

The knock on the door sounded like someone was using a brick. Mrs Gladstone folded those skinny arms of hers and said, 'Well, here we go.'

'I'll see who's there, ma'am.'

'I know who's there. If you don't open that door, she's just going to knock it down.'

The knock came louder.

'Coming,' I said, moving quickly to the door. I opened it and looked down at a very attractive grey-haired woman in a white suit and a crisp yellow blouse and Spectator pumps. She patted down her straw hat with the navy ribbon and shook my hand hard. This woman had a grip.

'Alice Lovett,' she announced. 'Retired shoe model.'

'Uh . . . Jenna Boller. Teen driver.'

Alice Lovett marched into the room, took one look at Mrs Gladstone and said, 'Madeline, you look like the devil himself. I'm going to feel sorry for you whether you like it or not.'

'I don't like it,' Mrs Gladstone spat.

'Tough cahoonas,' Alice Lovett spat back, took off her

hat, and sat down on the chair near the bed. I figured she was pushing seventy, which is probably the only way to approach that age. She looked like an ad for an older person's personal product, like Depends or Metamucil, that wants everyone to believe that no matter how old a human being gets they can still live a good life even if their waste disposal system goes south.

'Mrs Lovett, can I get you something to drink?'

Her face got hard. 'Everyone calls me Alice! I don't answer to anything else!'

'Sorry . . .' I backed off to the corner.

'Madeline, what can I do for you?' Alice demanded.

Mrs Gladstone sat there for the longest time without saying anything as Alice stared at her. Finally, 'I suppose, Alice, you can listen.'

Alice kicked off her size 5½ white and blue Spectator pumps, stuck her feet on the bed, and listened. Mrs Gladstone told her everything.

'Your own son!' Alice said and studied Mrs Gladstone's wrinkled face. Mrs Gladstone tried staring back at her like nothing was wrong, but Alice wouldn't let her. She inched up close. 'Madeline, I've known you for forty-one years and every one of them's been a challenge. I've seen you go to work with a one hundred-and-four degree fever. I've watched you collapse from exhaustion after weeks of eighteen-hour days. I've seen you refuse to cry at your own husband's funeral. But I want you to answer me the way it really is: can you make it to Texas?'

Mrs Gladstone sat as straight as she could.

'Well, of course I can!'

Alice yanked on her Spectators, patted down her hat. 'I'd say, Madeline, that's mostly bull. But, you know me, honey, I've always liked a good fight. I'm coming with you. But first Jenna and I are going to get you a wheelchair.'

Mrs Gladstone reared up like a wild horse. '*I will not sit in one of*—'

Alice Lovett, retired shoe model, put her hands on her hips like Mrs Gladstone was a dog who'd just messed the rug. 'You haven't got a whole lot to say about it.'

Sticking Mrs Gladstone in a wheelchair and expecting her to cooperate was like plopping a chicken in a church pew and telling it not to squawk.

'I will walk to the elevator!' Mrs Gladstone shouted.

Alice planted her feet in front of the elevator door and stood tough. 'Madeline, you hush!'

I turned away so they wouldn't see me laughing. Mrs Gladstone had met her match and it was doing me a whole lot of good.

Alice looked at me. 'Have you ever thought of wearing bangs, Jenna?'

I put my hand self-consciously over my forehead. 'No.'

'Bangs would frame your eyes. You have very nice eyes.'

Alice studied me like I was incomplete. 'And more green,' she said. 'You ought to wear more green with your hair.' My grandmother used to tell me that.

'Green's hard to find,' I muttered, feeling ugly.

The elevator door opened. 'Not always,' Alice said and pushed Mrs Gladstone inside. We rode to the main lobby in silence. When the door opened, Elden Gladstone, Shoe Rodent, was there to greet us.

Fourteen

'WHAT'S ALL THIS, MOTHER?'

Elden glared at his mother in the wheelchair without so much as a how-are-you.

Mrs Gladstone sat straight and proud and didn't skip a beat. 'My hip's acting up, Elden. Nice of you to ask.'

Elden took a deep breath. 'Are you all right?'

'That depends on how you define all right.'

'Does it *hurt?*' he asked impatiently.

'Not as much as other things,' she said, staring right back at him.

He looked away. 'We need to talk, Mother. You need to hear me out.'

'I'm due in Kansas City,' she said, motioning to me to start pushing. Elden stood in her path.

'This conversation needs to happen!' Elden insisted. He looked at me like I was a spy with hidden recording equipment. *'Alone.'*

'I'm afraid that's impossible,' Mrs Gladstone said.

Alice and I dug in our spurs and tried to look mean.

Elden knelt down by the wheelchair. I didn't think he had it in him. He put both his hands on the wheelchair arms and smiled like a used car salesman. 'Mother, you know my feelings on how business could be better.'

Mrs Gladstone's face got stiff.

'Not that business isn't good. It could just be spectacular. And you know how the Shoe Warehouse, which is a highly profitable venture, Mother, despite your concerns—'

Mrs Gladstone reared up. '*Their merchandise is atrocious!*'

'*They give the public what it wants!*'

Beads of sweat were popping on Elden's pale forehead. 'Mother, Ken Woldman of the Shoe Warehouse, who is one of the hottest retail deal-makers going, wants to buy Gladstone's for a great deal of *cash*.' He said 'cash' like she was hard of hearing. 'We would like your blessing to go ahead and—'

'Change the very fabric of the company.' Mrs Gladstone stirred in the wheelchair, enraged.

'Mother, this is how business is done now. It's not the same world you and Dad knew. The shoe business is changing and Gladstone's has to change with it to survive. This opportunity is being handed to us on a silver platter. It will send the stock soaring. We will all make a killing!'

Mrs Gladstone looked like she was going to crack Elden over the head with her cane.

I said, 'Mrs Gladstone, should I help you into the bathroom so you can take your medicine?'

Her jaw clenched.

'Remember what the doctor said, ma'am.' I rolled her toward the ladies' room, a vermin-free zone.

The doctor hadn't said anything about bathrooms, but Mrs Gladstone got my drift. I pushed her inside. 'I don't think this is what Mr Bender would want you to do.'

Her hand gripped the sink in anger.

'Mr Bender said to just be polite and not give any information and not to slap a man who's chewing tobacco.' She looked at me irritated. 'It sounds better when he says it.'

'All right. All right.'

'Maybe you could smile, ma'am.'

She cracked her mouth open like she had a toothache. Alice walked in, shaking her head.

I said, 'You need to work on the smile, Mrs Gladstone. It isn't enough to let your teeth show, you've got to look like you mean it.'

Alice whipped a big red lipstick from her purse and put it on. 'Madeline, this child speaks the truth. If you can't smile at what's going on, think of something else that'll make you happy, and smile at that. I did that through most of my second marriage.'

'I can't think of anything that will make me happy.'

'Think about Harry Bender and how he's going to help you,' I suggested.

She grunted. I wheeled her back out with Alice guarding the rear.

Elden was pacing, checking his gold watch.

Mrs Gladstone said, 'Well, Elden as you can see, I'm just doing poorly. We'd better postpone this until I'm stronger.'

Elden didn't like that. 'There are decisions that need to be made!'

Alice and I stared at her. *Smile.*

She did, sort of. 'Well, of course there are, dear. Just give me a little time. This medicine I'm on makes me so woozy.' She flopped back in the chair, closed her eyes.

'For crying out loud, Mother, you're seventy-three years old! You've done fine things for this company, but it's time to let the next generation take the reins. I'll call you in a few days!'

Elden flipped open his portable phone and stormed out. Mrs Gladstone watched him push through the lobby door, rush out onto the street. She was trying so hard to be brave, her face looked like it was carved from granite. She caught Alice and me looking at her.

'I'm fine!' she spat.

Some people just never let down.

'Madeline,' Alice announced, pushing the wheelchair forwards, 'you are many things right now, but fine is not one of them.'

I steered the Cadillac towards Kansas City. Mrs Gladstone was sleeping in the backseat. Alice was humming, lost in thought. I passed a slow-moving station wagon and clicked into the freedom of driving.

My father used to talk about being on the road, selling. Every day a new city. You've got to smile when you meet the people. I remember him standing at the bathroom mirror shaving, getting himself pumped for a trip. There was a rhythm to it.

Shake hands.

Stay hungry.

Stay focused.

They can't say no.

Push through till the end of the day.

Nobody buys from a loser.

Another room.

Another restaurant.

Another piece of road just like the next.

Go first class.

Deal at the top.

Never let them see you sweat.

Keep driving.

Cars were important to Dad. He got a new one each year. I remember how he'd pull up to our house, honking like mad, and I'd run out and see the new red machine. They were always red. Mustangs, Thunderbirds. Dad liked things sporty. 'First thing a customer sees about me is the car I drive,' Dad always said. Dad took care of his cars, too. Waxed them each week, wiped them down, got the oil changed on time, the tune-ups. He took better care of those cars than he did his family.

I guess people take special care of the things that are important to them.

I tried my best to be important to my father. I didn't argue with him, even when I knew he was wrong. I didn't call him a drunk, even though he was one. I just tiptoed around his life, hoping he'd notice. He did sometimes, but he'd be gone in a heartbeat, off chasing some scheme that was going to make him rich. He'd say how all the people who didn't believe in him would sure look stupid when he came out on top.

Dad said that money talked. And when he had it, he spread it around – buying things we didn't need, like fur coats and fancy jewellery for Mom, leaving big tips. I realized later it was how he tried to get people to love him.

The stairway in our first house had a hand-carved rail. If you weren't careful, you could get splinters if you slid your hand down it too fast. Faith got splinters in her rear end once; she didn't try that again. The rail curled to a landing just before you'd get upstairs. I remember that stairway more than my room. That's where I'd sit and watch when my father would come home drunk. I'd hear the car pull up, the door slam shut, Dad clear his throat, spit on the sidewalk. I'd climb out of bed and huddle on the landing. I don't know why. He'd slam through the door, grab at the striped wall to keep standing. Mom would meet him or not, depending. Once he saw me watching from the landing, sitting on the hope chest in my nightgown.

'Whatch you looking at?' he shouted and then vomited on the rug.

Daddy's home.

Fifteen

KANSAS CITY. NINE-THIRTY AM. I DROPPED MRS
Gladstone off at the downtown Kansas City store. I
was supposed to wait twenty minutes and then come in to
snoop.

I parked the Cadillac, slipped out in spy fashion.
Looked around. Typical shopping district. Kansas City
didn't seem like a big city, it was more like a community of
little towns. I walked slowly down the street, whistling an
undercover tune, stopped at a magazine stand searching
for clues. Saw the cover of *Business Week* magazine.

'The rise of Ken Woldman, Wall Street shoe baron,'
blared the headline.

Pretty good clue.

I bought the magazine (know thy enemy), sauntered
out. Hit the coffee bar. Got a decaf latte, grabbed a stool,
turned to the article and Ken Woldman's tanned, rich,
smiling face – a face that said: Worship me. I know about
money.

I started reading. Ken Woldman had taken Wall Street
by storm in only five short years as the Shoe Warehouse
broke records for sales and profitability. 'A good price is
what people want today in shoes and anything else,' he
was quoted. 'You give them the right price, they give you
their business.'

He was thirty-two years old and lived in Nebraska. He
was a quiet, energetic man, who only needed three hours

of sleep each night. There was a picture of him at three AM in his office, practicing golf putts in front of a huge map of the world. There was a picture of him and his wife – she had dark circles under her eyes, probably from being married to all that energy. He was tall and impossibly thin and had a computer in every room of his fourteen-room mansion including the bathrooms. He called himself "a numbers man who can anticipate the market." His motto: believe in yourself, then tell the world.

I sipped my latte.

Read on about how the Shoe Warehouse had grown by buying and selling companies, making big profits. Giving the public what it wants: decent shoes at warehouse prices.

And all this time I thought the public wanted great shoes at fair prices.

I kept reading, hoping something would be said about quality, but quality was never mentioned. I guess that's not how Wall Street measures success.

I checked my watch mysteriously.

Time to spy.

I stood in the middle of the downtown Kansas City Gladstone's and felt like I was in an elegant house that had been decorated with cheap furniture.

The ceiling of the store arched upward like a church, but below it were rows of tall metal display cases with so-so shoes on sale. The Gladstone's sign looked out of place and the Texas Lone Star on the wall seemed embarrassed. Lots of shoppers were trying on shoes, but there wasn't any energy in the place. I tried on a pair of leather tie-ons that looked promising; wiggled my toes. Passable, but not great. I took them off. Murray would never settle for passable.

WE'RE NOT JUST SELLING SHOES, WE'RE SELLING QUALITY the sign proclaimed.

Two women went to the small sitting area where a sales-person could help them. Only the manager was on the floor and she was busy at the register. I looked at Mrs Gladstone. When you've driven 600 miles with a person, you can communicate across a room.

'Jenna's with me, Cynthia,' Mrs Gladstone said to the manager. 'She can help those customers.'

Cynthia looked at me unsure.

I took my initialled shoehorn out of my pocket, walked to the women. 'How can I help you today?'

They looked at me gratefully. I smiled back. Trust moved between us.

The blonde woman's problem was basic – she wore too tight shoes and they were causing corns on the tops of her toes. Some people are so used to feeling bad they think it's normal.

'I can help you with that,' I told her, 'but you need to try a new look, something that won't pinch so much.'

I got her into low-heeled leather walkers that would take the punishment of everyday use but still look nice; found her a lower-cut, squared toe pump that didn't rub against her skinny ankles. Then I showed the grey-haired woman a Stride-Rite pump that she could almost jog in, a supershoe for business-women on the go. She took three of those in black, camel, and blush vino. Told her nonjudgmentally to think about clipping her big toenail so it wouldn't push against the shoe and ruin the fit.

'Fit is everything, ma'am,' I said as I walked them to the cash register, having sold five pairs of quality shoes in under ten mintues. They danced out of the store with happy feet.

I blew on my shoehorn to cool it down, tossed it in the air in a little twirl, and put it back in my pocket.

The days blended together.

Kansas City.

Topeka.

Wichita.

Oklahoma City.

Fort Smith.

Little Rock.

So many stores to see, so many miles to cover. After a while, everything started looking alike. Thirty-five South looked like 40 East. Arkansas looked like Kansas.

Keep pushing.

Eat, sleep, drive, spy.

I learned great road truths that teenagers aren't always exposed to.

Never go into a restaurant with a sign that says GOOD EATS.

Never eat at a place called MOM'S, because it's a safe bet Mom's been dead for years and whoever's in the kitchen didn't have a working relationship with her.

If you see four or more pickups in front of a diner, chances are you'll get a good meal.

I got Mrs Gladstone and Alice to start slumming it more and we found some excellent down-and-dirty restaurants – but the corn beef hash, fried eggs, and mile-high cinnamon rolls at the Road to Nowhere Truck Stop redefined breakfast as we know it. An old trucker fell in love with Alice and kept sending her love notes at our table. She blushed and grinned and kept every one. 'That man,' she'd say, rereading the notes, 'if he knew how old I was!'

We'd pull off the road to read historical markers and then Mrs Gladstone would talk about some piece of shoe history that nobody ever heard of like how the first saddle shoes were made in 1906 for tennis and squash players; how the earliest known shoes were sandals and archae-ologists found a pair in Egypt made of papyrus braiding that are 4,000 years old.

I learned that every driver on the road *thinks* they drive well, but like Alice said, thinking and doing are two different animals.

I saw that kindness is still alive and well in America when an old woman paid our fifty-cent bridge toll and waved to us as she drove by.

I realized that helping a family put the mattress back on the roof of their car after it blew off in the wind looks a whole lot easier than it is.

We hit every rest stop known to man, checked in and out of too many hotels, and found the best deep dish cherry pie in America at Pearlie Mae's Roadside Diner. You'd never think a dump like that could offer something so perfect. I saw teenagers in cars, but hadn't talked to one for weeks. You know you've been with old people too long when you can pick out the subtle differences between Count Basie's and Duke Ellington's piano playing.

And then there was the business.

Harry Bender was calling stockholders and was hitting one brick wall after the other. Lots of them wanted Gladstone's to stay like it was, but Elden's promise of soaring stock prices with the Shoe Warehouse sale got people looking at their wallets instead of in their hearts.

Elden kept calling Mrs Gladstone.

Mrs Gladstone kept hedging, telling Elden she couldn't talk. Every time she did, she sounded tougher and Alice would shout, 'Welcome back, tiger. You're sounding like your old self.'

We pushed on. It was August now. The summer heat could slap you unconscious with its strength. We hit awful construction on 40 East in Arkansas that makes you hate the whole world – cars sat backed up for miles while some guy with a cement truck tried to manoeuver around a line of angry, honking motorists who were shouting and swearing like Chicago cab drivers. Then the funniest thing happened.

Mrs Gladstone started getting stronger.

You couldn't tell at first, her being so gruff and all, but after we left Little Rock where the manager gave her the biggest hug you've ever seen and told her how much working for her had meant to him, told her how he'd learned more at Gladstone's than anyplace else, told her how, as a stockholder, he wasn't going to vote for the sale to go through and he knew plenty of other people who felt the same way. The more stores we saw, the stronger Mrs Gladstone got. Store owners were telling her they loved her, and halfway to Shreveport Mrs Gladstone started walking on her own, and when I asked what I should do with the wheelchair she got a spark in her eye and said she didn't give a 'blasted bloody rip.'

Mrs Gladstone and Alice started talking about how senior citizens were getting pushed aside in America and how older people had to start fighting back. By the time we'd crossed Mississippi into Louisiana, I thought I had a revolution on my hands because they were shouting about all their combined wisdom and experience not being appreciated and what this world needed was to bring some seniors out of retirement to whip everyone into shape.

We headed for the Shreveport store and Mrs Gladstone and Alice weren't going to take any guff. Alice had a coupon for free stewed prunes at Buster's Breakfast Café and Laundromat and when she tried to redeem it after she'd eaten the prunes the waitress said she could only use it in Arkansas, which caused Alice to shoot up like a firecracker, shouting that old people were getting harassed and pushed out in America and she wasn't going to take it anymore. Alice shoved her prune coupon in the waitress's face.

'In China a person doesn't become respected for their

wisdom until they reach seventy years of age and I guarantee you, I qualify!'

The waitress stepped back and said Alice could have the prunes and Alice said good, she wasn't giving them back except the hard way.

I pushed on to Shreveport, being extra careful not to get any old people irritated.

At the Shreveport store, Alice and Mrs Gladstone surrounded the manager, Big Bob Capshaw, who was telling Mrs Gladstone how Elden's new merchandise was the best thing going and it was a privilege to sell it.

'You think my brain's turned to mush?' Mrs Gladstone asked him.

'No . . . no, ma'am.'

'Darn straight,' Alice added, stomping her size 5½ pumps.

'You're standing in the presence of fifty golden years of shoe selling expertise,' Mrs Gladstone informed him.

Big Bob Capshaw wiped his brow. 'I don't want any trouble, ma'am. I've lost three jobs in four years. I just try to sell what gets sent to me.'

'You getting any complaints on those shoes?' Mrs Gladstone demanded.

'I've . . . well, we've had a few more than usual.'

'How many more?'

He gulped. 'You want me to get the exact numbers?'

Mrs Gladstone rammed her cane on the counter. 'I want every sale, return, and profit and loss figure you've got in this store.'

Big Bob hurried off.

Alice did a little jig. 'Madeline, I swear, I feel fifty!'

Big Bob came back with the books. Mrs Gladstone pored over them, asking him a hundred questions.

'What's the profit and loss on this brand?'

'What's your monthly return ratio?'

'What's your damaged goods number for the quarter?'

She took notes in her blue leather book; slammed it shut. 'You've got quite a system going here, don't you? Buying low-end merchandise, selling it cheaper than our regular prices, but higher than it's worth. No returns for cash. And all in this quarter, too. You've made a lot of money, Bob.' She leaned forward, her grey eyes on fire. 'Now what in the blue blazes can we make of that?'

'Mrs Gladstone,' he began—

She wasn't having any. *Isn't this a fine way to make Gladstone's look more profitable for that fancy takeover?* She reared up. *How many customers who count on our quality have been snookered?*

Big Bob was looking smaller. 'Mrs Gladstone, this isn't illegal, it's just . . . business.'

'It's immoral! Shame on you! Shame on you all!'

She grabbed her cane, whacked the counter, and stormed out the door.

Big Bob was shaking in his boots.

Alice grabbed his shiny lapel. 'We'll be watching, *junior.*'

By the time we zoomed onto Interstate 20 heading west to Dallas, we had more horsepower in the backseat than we did under the hood. And that sleazy man pumping gas at the Mobil rest stop rued the day he was born when he tried to cheat Mrs Gladstone out of the change she had coming, telling her she'd given him thirty dollars not forty. Mrs Gladstone sprung out of the car swinging her cane.

'I gave you two twenties!' she shouted. 'You can give me my proper change now or when the police come.'

She got her change, but she still wasn't satisfied. She shoved her cane right under his chin. 'Don't mess with seniors,' she growled at him. I burned a little rubber out of the station and leaned on the horn just to make sure he got the message.

Finally I passed a road sign that read, WELCOME TO TEXAS – DRIVE FRIENDLY. If I'd been wearing a hat I would have taken it off and thrown it in the air. Alice yelled, *'Yeeehaaa!'* Mrs Gladstone rolled down her window to breathe in the Texas oxygen.

Was it my imagination, or did everyone on the road suddenly start driving faster?

Sixteen

*I*T WASN'T MY IMAGINATION.

Pickups raced past me. The right hand mirror with the little sign, "Objects you see are closer than they appear," was making me nervous because a large Chevy Suburban was barrelling very close in that mirror like a lion hunting down an injured gazelle. Drive like everyone around you is crazy, Mom always said.

They were crazy. I gripped the wheel and tried a driving trick my grandmother used to use. When she was stressed behind the wheel, she'd make the other drivers around her seem real. She'd ask herself what they did for a living, what kind of lives did they lead?

A vicious truck vroomed ahead of me – "Don't Mess with Texas" the bumper sticker read.

How could this gentleman support himself?

Gun runner?

Prison guard?

It was a hundred miles to Dallas. I got in the far right lane that was only going fourteen miles over the speed limit. I did my best to stay legal.

One twenty to the LBJ Freeway.

US 175 to 130.

Cars with bumper stickers zoomed by:

"Native Texan."

"Naturalized Texan."

"Purebread Texan."

"Texan by Choice."

Mrs Gladstone was saying how just being on Texas soil always got her blood pumping. It seemed to have this effect on other people, too.

'I thought people in Texas were laid back,' I shouted as two mega-trucks thundered by.

'They are,' Mrs Gladstone said happily, 'except on the road.'

I sat tall and drove; the Cadillac's wheels were eating up the pavement.

And then Dallas signs and street names hit from left to right, and there in front of me was the Emerald City, except it wasn't green. It was gold and shiny. Huge skyscrapers (not as big as Chicago, but I wasn't complaining) pushed to the big sky.

I shook off tiredness and took it all in. Mrs Gladstone and Alice were trying to find Pegasus, the flying red horse on top of the Magnolia Building. They were pointing out the NationsBank Plaza that was seventy-two floors high, the Trinity River that flowed underneath the freeways.

I drove on, yielding to hordes of speeding drivers.

Alice said she'd read an article that said men were three times as likely to be in an accident than women, which didn't surprise any of us. A male-driven convertible appeared out of nowhere and cut in front of me without signalling. I gave him acres of room. Have your accident somewhere else, sir.

Finally, I pulled onto the tree-lined streets of Highland Park, a rich Dallas suburb with big-time houses. Minutes later I turned into Mrs Gladstone's long, curling driveway.

Her huge white ranch house hugged the driveway with an attached greenhouse that my mother would have loved. A wide porch wrapped around the front with hanging plants and rocking chairs. All the windows were tall and glistening. The house stretched before us like it had been there forever, like nothing could ever knock it down. A gardener was watering cascading roses that hung over a trestle. He smiled and waved; his gold front tooth gleamed in the sun. I pulled to a stop. Alice was saying, 'Oh, Madeline, you've done so much with the garden.'

That's when Elden drove up behind us in his green Mercedes.

'Well,' said Mrs Gladstone. 'Looks like things are going to get interesting.'

Elden stood at his mother's side of the car. She pressed a button. Her window rolled down.

'Mother, we have to talk.' He eyed me coldly.

He was a real ace at killing a mood. The gardener stopped smiling. I wondered what it was like to never have anyone happy to see you.

'I'd like to take a look around the house first, Elden. Then we can talk.'

'I'm sick of these games, Mother.' He opened the car door.

'What a coincidence,' she said, pushing him aside with her cane. 'So am I.'

He watched her get out of the car. 'What happened to the wheelchair?'

'Oh, that old thing,' said Mrs Gladstone walking off with her cane.

I said, 'Hello, sir,' and got the luggage from the trunk. I'd driven 1,532 miles and didn't feel like being greeted in the Promised Land by a retail turncoat. Alice got out, too, said, 'Well . . . Elden,' and caught up with Mrs Gladstone who was talking to the gardener, telling him what a fine job he had done with the flowers. The gardener was so proud and was pointing out the new plantings as she and Alice walked around the grounds. Elden was ready to pop but Mrs Gladstone took her time hobbling, admiring nature's blessings. Elden's blood pressure hit full boil. I grinned happily.

A woman in a maid's uniform opened the front door. I carried the luggage inside the house and gasped. Floor-to-ceiling windows, big overstuffed beige sofas, cream-coloured walls, huge paintings of flowers, horse sculptures.

Elden and Mrs Gladstone followed me inside. He said, 'Mother, sit down.'

She did and motioned me to sit next to her.

'Mother, this is a confidential business discussion. I hardly think that your *driver* can add anything noteworthy.'

I could kick you in the stomach, I thought, moving towards the couch. I could drag you across Texas by your pointy ears.

Mrs Gladstone smiled at me. 'She's my *assistant*, Elden.'

I sucked in my stomach proudly. Jenna Boller, assistant to the president. Had a nice ring to it. Maybe more money.

Mrs Gladstone folded her arms. 'Now what did you want to say?'

'Mother, I insist on this being a private conversation.'

'Why?'

'Because I'm your son.'

She leaned forward and raised an angry hand. 'You have gone behind my back, you have gone to my board of directors to try to overthrow me, you have sought to make deals with this company you had no right to negotiate, you have been dishonest, disreputable, and devious. You have not earned the right, *my son*, to speak with me privately.'

The colour drained from Elden's face until he perfectly

matched the sofa. He clenched his jaw until I thought blood would drip out.

'*Everything* I have done, Mother, was for the financial good of this company.'

'That's manure!'

Elden stood up fast. 'We see things differently, you and I. You see some grand moral plan that sells shoes like they're the cure for cancer. They're shoes, Mother. *Just shoes*. Maybe you and Dad needed to think of them as something more. And that's fine. But in the real world, it doesn't matter if you're selling shoes, or widgets, or Lear jets. What matters is the bottom line. How much you make. What the company's worth. How to get the stock up. And you're kidding yourself if you think business is anything more than that!'

'I would not be in business if I thought that was all it was about!'

Elden slammed his hands to his side.'That's why it's time for you to retire. That's why the board will accept your resignation, hands down. It's over. The stockholders want the takeover, we will make a great deal of money. Our profits this quarter have been terrific. Take your millions and have a ball!'

'How do you account for those fourth quarter profits?'

'Smart merchandising, Mother. Just taking the company to the next level.'

Mrs Gladstone looked at him hard. 'What about quality?'

He picked at his manicured nail. 'Not many people can tell a well-made shoe these days. Decent sells well enough.'

'*I can tell!*' Her eyes blasted through him. Elden looked away. 'If your father was alive—'

'He'd thank me! Dad was a salesman. He understood the bottom line. There are no guarantees out there anywhere, and I'll tell you, that scares me. So when I can turn a fat profit, I'm going to do it to protect my future and—'

'Get out,' Mrs Gladstone whispered.

'Now look, Mother, I know you're upset, but—'

'Get out.' She said the next part quietly. 'Jenna will see you to the door.'

I stood super tall and looked down at Elden like he was fertilizer. I wished I was wearing one of those Kung Fu robes and could stand by the couch and do high kicks like a bodyguard.

He reared up. 'I will not be pushed out by some *giant*—'

Mrs Gladstone rammed her old hand hard on the thick wood coffee table. *'Be very careful of your words!'*

Elden stormed towards the door, saying he could find his own way out. I followed him, in case he was as stupid as he looked. He opened the door, glared up at me.

'I don't like your game,' he hissed, his pasty face getting pink. 'And just in case you haven't heard, *no one* pushes me around.'

Seventeen

*H*ARRY BENDER, THE WORLD'S GREATEST SHOE salesman, bent over the Bass shoe display at the downtown Dallas Gladstone's, which was, without question, the biggest shoe store I had ever seen. It had three floors – men's, women's, and children's – and a huge white spiral staircase that wrapped around the largest plastic foot in the universe, with toes that started by the Johnston and Murphy display and a leg that reached to the sky past the women's squared-toe flats. Everything is bigger in Texas.

Harry was about my size. He was wearing handstitched Tony Lama snakeskin cowboy boots and a very large Stetson hat. His starched white shirt was open at the neck – no tie. He had the kind of face you could picture laying in the sewer someplace after getting beat up.

'Now this one here,' he held up a leather walker to the man he was waiting on, 'this one's got everything you need. Good traction, hugs the road.'

'Sounds like a tyre,' the man said, amused.

'Better than a tyre. This old shoe'll take you places a tyre only dreamed of.'

'Eleven D,' the man said, smiling.

Harry Bender tipped his hat to me and Mrs Gladstone and hustled into the back and came out moments later with a box.

'See,' Harry was saying, putting the shoe on the man,

lacing it up. 'Most folks don't treat their feet right. They just take shoes for granted. I tell you shoes can turn a life around. Twenty-three years ago I was drunk and out of work and so broke I was wearing bedroom slippers. But a priest took pity on me and got me a pair of soft leather tie-ons. I figured then and there that God was telling me to straighten up and sell shoes or join the priesthood.'

'I see the shoes won,' the man said, chuckling.

'Well, the Lord knew I'd given my wife enough guff. The priesthood would of blown her cork clear to Amarillo.'

The man was laughing, standing up in the Basses. 'They feel good,' he said, wiggling his toes.

'Yeah, those'll do you a good turn. You want to wear 'em or carry 'em?'

'I'll keep them on.'

'Mr Rodriguez,' Harry Bender bellowed happily at a moustached man behind the counter, 'get this fine gentleman checked out so he can go back to celebrating the good life God gave him.'

Everyone in the store was grinning. Some people just naturally make you glad to be alive.

Harry Bender raced up to Mrs Gladstone and grabbed her two bony hands in his big hairy ones. 'Blast, Maddy, it's good to see you.'

Mrs Gladstone looked at him beaming. 'You making me rich, Harry?'

He patted her hands. 'Every day, old girl.' Harry Bender grinned at me. He had the most genuine smile I'd ever seen, not a scrap of fakeness in it. 'You must be Jenna.' He put his hand out to me. 'Welcome to Texas.'

We ate lunch with Harry Bender and he was putting away as much Texas barbecue as a human being could and still be conscious: brisket, pinto beans, sausage, Texas toast.

He was wearing a lapel pin, 'Live each day as though it's your last,' but I didn't think it was referring to food consumption. The restaurant had long tables covered with paper, and the man carving the brisket shouted 'Señor Bender!' when we walked in and sliced us the best pieces of meat, using that knife of his like a sculptor. It was the best barbecue I'd ever tasted, which reminded me of the B minus I got last year on a history paper that should have been an A-minus easy. The topic was, What are the things America will be remembered for? I wrote baseball, jazz, barbecue, and the Constitution. Mr Hellritter wrote "Limited" across the top of my essay in red pen, which I guess I should have expected, him being a vegetarian. Opal is a vegetarian except when barbecue is around. She says barbecue is a food group unto itself. That's one of the things I like about her. She doesn't fight it when the lines blur.

Harry Bender and Mrs Gladstone had moved from talking about Elden to talking about the good old days.

'This man,' Mrs Gladstone was laughing, 'came to our Dallas store twenty-three years ago insisting we hire him even though he had no experience.'

'You were the biggest thing in town, Maddy. I figured why waste my talent in some joint?'

'What were you doing before, sir?'

'I was a ranch hand in Forth Worth; went from place to place pretty much.'

I could see him wrestling cows to the ground.

'Yeah, I stormed right in, told Floyd it was his lucky day, God had sent me. He hired me on the spot. Haven't had a drink since.'

I smiled. 'You make it sound easy.'

'Staying sober is the hardest thing I do. Sometimes I'm with someone who's drinking and feeling happy and I start thinking I can handle it now. I can have one.

Then I remember what a fat lie that is. I can't handle a drop.'

Mr Bender's cell phone started ringing. He flipped it open. 'You got Harry,' he said into the receiver.

He listened, covered the phone with his hand. 'One of the fellas I sponsor in AA,' he whispered to me and Mrs Gladstone. 'He's new at being sober. Gets the jitters sometimes.'

Mrs Gladstone patted my hand and excused herself to go to the bathroom. Harry Bender rammed his toothpick on the table. 'No, no, no,' he said into the phone. 'You know if you take a drink you're not going to be able to stop.'

He listened some more.

'I know how hard it is, but you can't get near that stuff. It's poison in your life and the Lord couldn't have made that more clear if he'd hung you by your toes over a manure pile. You listen to me, old boy, and throw it out now . . . I know it . . . I know it . . . all right . . . call back if you need to.'

Harry closed his phone, stuck it back on his belt.

'That's great you sponsor people, Mr Bender.'

'That's what it's about. Had some fine men help me years ago. Just trying to return the favour.'

I took a deep breath. 'Boy . . . I, um . . . I wish you could talk to my father. He . . .'

'Hits the sauce?'

'Yeah,' I said quietly.

'Your dad at a point where he wants to talk?'

'No.'

He sniffed. 'You getting help for yourself?'

I told him about Al-Anon and the way we talked about things in my family.

'Best thing you can do for your dad is love him and pray for him and don't let him step on you or let his disease infect you any more than it has.'

'I try.'

'So many hurting people,' Harry Bender said, looking out the window. 'I'll tell you what, though, if you set your mind and heart toward a healthy way of living and thinking, you'll find a way to climb out of the biggest pit life throws your way.'

He flipped his Stetson back on his head and smiled.

I didn't say what I was thinking.

How I wished he was my father.

Eighteen

I SAT ON THE WHITE BED IN THE ALL-WHITE GUEST
room in Mrs Gladstone's house and really felt like a
visitor. It was the kind of room that forced you to make the
bed and pick up your dirty clothes even though it was
against your nature. I hugged my knees and wondered
what it would have been like if Harry Bender had been my
father.

I saw him taking me out in the backyard when I was
small and teaching me all about shoes.

I saw him feeding me little bites of barbecue when I was
a baby.

Mostly I saw him just being there – someone you could
count on who shot hoops with you after dinner. Someone
who came to your school plays even though you were
playing non-speaking tall parts, like trees and giant
lizards. Someone who understood that what kids need
most from their fathers is for them to be available and
loving.

I curled under the covers and opened the letter my
mother had sent me. "Hello out there," it began.

I have told Faith she cannot have your room, despite the
fact that she offered me money. I suppose we all have our
price, but she was going to have to do a whole lot better
than twenty-seven dollars.

We are shouldering work, life, and Chicago humidity

with the usual grace and sophistication. I'm working too hard as usual. People continue to do stupid things to themselves and others, so, sadly, business in the emergency room is booming. I wonder sometimes if I'm seeing such a jaded part of life here day after day that it muddies my view of humanity. Part of me longs for a normal job, but I've tried to drop normal from my vocabulary because I have come to the conclusion, rightly or wrongly, that there is no such thing.

I wonder what you are learning and seeing on the road, Jenna. Knowing you, it will be quite a lot. I hope that part of this trip is bringing you peace and understanding in addition to the much-needed time away.

On a more complex note, I need to tell you that we've had to change our phone number to an unlisted one because your father has been calling late at night and he's not been in the best form. I know this is hard news to hear when you're away, but for safety's sake I wanted you to have our new number – 555-7790. It will be installed next week. Faith is handling this, so am I. It's unfortunate that your dad's problems continue, but for now an unlisted number seems to be the best way for us to deal with them.

Don't worry about us, Jenna. We're doing fine. If you want to talk, you can call me at home or at the hospital. I think of you a dozen times each day and wish you grace, strength, and wisdom on your journey.

Love, always,
Mom

A sickening anxiety washed over me. I looked at the white phone on the bedside table. I tried to swallow; I couldn't. I felt a panic take hold.

I shouldn't have left.

I had to call her. I reached for the phone. My hand froze above the receiver.

I closed my eyes and remembered myself as a little girl.

The phone rang. Dad was drunk, told me to answer it; say he wasn't home.

'I don't want to, Daddy.'

'Do it.'

I walked to it slowly, hoping it would stop ringing before I got there.

No such luck.

'Hello?' I said, small and scared.

'I'm looking for Jim Boller.' It was always an angry voice.

I gulped. Looked at my father, who was staring at me. 'He's . . . not here.'

'When will he be back?' the voice demanded.

'I . . . I don't know.'

'Can you take a message?'

'I can't write good yet.'

Click. The angry voice hung up.

I stood there like someday my lying was going to catch up with me.

'Good girl,' Dad said. 'That wasn't so bad, right?'

I ran into the other room to play with my plastic animals that I kept in a box under my bed. Once Grandma got me a miniature phone so my animals could talk on it, but I gave it back to her because the animals didn't like it.

I shook the memory from my mind, grabbed the phone near the bed, punched buttons, waited, hoping I wouldn't sound as nervous as I felt.

The hospital receptionist switched me to the ER and finally I got Mom.

'We're fine, honey,' was the first thing she said.

I could hear someone groaning in the background, the sound of racing footsteps.

'You're busy,' I said, feeling stiff.

'A car accident.' I knew she couldn't talk.

'Do you want me to come home Mom?'

'Of course not.'

'Is Dad . . . all right? I don't think he means to do these things.'

'Right now, Jenna, I'm just dealing with the fact that he does them.'

I could hear a man say, 'Carol, we need you.'

'Be right there,' Mom said. 'Can I call you tomorrow, Jenna? Are you all right?'

'I'm OK. I don't know where I'll be tomorrow.'

'Carol!' said the man insistently.

'It's OK, Mom. We'll talk. I'll write you a long letter.'

'I love you, sweetie.'

'I love you, too.'

I didn't get to ask her about Grandma.

I sat on the bed holding the letter; the weight of it rolled over me. I thought about how Mom had crawled out from such a painful marriage, how she'd pushed herself to look at the things she needed to change.

'If you set your mind and heart toward a healthy way of living and thinking,' Harry Bender had said, 'you'll find a way to climb out of the biggest pit life throws your way.'

Then for some reason I saw myself as a little girl again.

The phone rang.

Dad told me to answer it; say he wasn't home.

This time I dug my red sneakers into the blue braided rug and said *no*.

Not this time, Daddy.

The next day Mrs Gladstone and I had a fight about her thinking I needed a day off and me saying I didn't.

'You need to rest!' she hollered. 'You've been on duty day and night.'

'I'm not too good at resting. It makes me nervous.'

'Now what in the world are you saying?'

Alice came out of the other guest room in the midst of it, looked me up and down like I needed fumigating, and held up a small pair of scissors.

'It's time, honey,' she said. 'You need bangs.'

'Um . . . no . . . I . . .'

But retired shoe models get pushy. She plopped me down on a bench in the hall in front of a floor-to-ceiling gold mirror. 'Just a few wispy bangs,' she said, lifting my hair off my shoulders and letting it fall. 'It'll frame your face so nicely; give you some softness. Won't hurt a bit.'

I said, 'I'm not sure about this,' as she parcelled out my hair over my forehead.

Alice stood back. 'I'm sure. I was the lead hairstylist at the Queen for a Day Beauty Salon and Nail Emporium for seven years before I went into shoe modelling. My customers begged me to stay, they were hanging onto my arms on my last day, weeping themselves silly. You'd have thought somebody died.'

I groaned, closed my eyes. I hated the sound of snipping scissors close to my face.

She snipped a bit, a bit more, stood back.

More still.

'I'm taking some off the sides,' she said, not asking. Hairdressers never do. If they touch your hair, they think they own it.

'Not much,' I pleaded.

She took some off the sides, some off the back to even it out. By the time she was done, I was close to being a different person.

'*Very* nice,' said Mrs Gladstone.

But Alice Lovett, retired shoe model wasn't satisfied. She dragged me out the door in search of green clothing.

Nineteen

'SUCK IT IN, HONEY.'

I sucked in my stomach and stood in front of a three-way mirror in the women's changing area of Northrop's Fashion Central, wearing a green shirt and a green checked skirt and a fat leather belt with a silver buckle that Alice had scooped from a fifty-per cent-off basket like a prospector finding a hunk of gold in a stream. I grinned.

Alice adjusted the belt, poufed the shirt out a bit. 'I always told my customers, the beginning of true beauty is how you feel inside.'

'I feel pretty good, Alice.'

'And that's radiating outward,' Alice said. 'Just look at that glow coming from you. It almost hurts my eyes.'

I did a little twirl in the skirt, laughing; the fabric lifted full and light over my knees.

'Green's the colour of new life,' Alice explained. 'It shows off your red hair, and those big belts work on tall women. You've got a good waist.'

I looked down happily at my waist. 'I do?'

'I couldn't wear a belt like that to save my pension.'

We found another green shirt, a few green sweaters. I kept looking at myself in store windows, in mirrors. I was so used to not looking. Sales clerks' eyes didn't cloud up when they waited on me. They kept eye contact, didn't look away. People always leaned closer to Faith when she was shopping.

When Alice and I returned to Mrs Gladstone's, I don't mind saying it, I looked great. My eyes seemed brighter, my face looked sparkly, my hair was close to perfect. Alice was being humble like all great miracle workers, saying she didn't do much, really.

Mrs Gladstone beamed at me and insisted I take the rest of the day off. 'Go,' she said, pushing me out the door. 'Clear your mind.'

'My mind doesn't work that way, Mrs Gladstone. It needs to have things in it.'

'*Go!*'

But where?

I drove downtown, sucking in my beauty. Matt Wicks didn't know what he was missing. Dallas is the second largest city in Texas, but I don't think it's a good idea to mention it to anyone living in Dallas. I was driving past the Dallas Public Library, thinking how Opal and I could make this day into a party. We'd walk into stores pretending we were rich, we'd make up stories about people we saw. Opal was always looking to have fun, even when it wasn't appropriate – like in school. School, I'd try to tell her, is about pain, pressure, and homework. But she'd never listen.

'The problem with you, Jenna,' she'd say, 'is you're too responsible.'

I guess she's right, but I don't think I can change.

I turned left and headed back towards the Dallas Public Library.

There was something I had to do.

I was sitting at a library study table. My grandma always said that God made libraries so that people didn't have any excuse to be stupid. Close to everything a human being needed to know was somewhere in the library.

There was plenty I needed to know.

I'd just typed 'Woldman, Ken' into the library computer, pressed 'Search,' and came up with five articles about him. I had them piled in front of me on the table and was studying his angular face on the cover of *Fortune* magazine, trying to figure out what he wanted with more shoe stores when he seemed to have enough already. I looked at Ken Woldman's blue eyes – bright like flames. He was looking right at me, it seemed, hands on his bony hips, shoulders shoved back. He didn't look like a man who would sell second-class shoes; second-class anything, for that matter. He seemed to wear his power easily, the way you toss a sweater over your shoulders on a summer night.

His father had been poor, the article said. Ken Woldman had three newspaper routes when he was a boy, a lawn-mowing service in high school that he still operates, giving students summer jobs. Before I worked at Gladstone's I did everything to make money – babysitting, dog walking, selling pennants and visors at Wrigley Field. *"Awwwwwright!"* I'd holler at the people filing in to watch the Chicago Cubs get slaughtered, *"Get your Cub memorabilia herrrrrrrrrre!"* But my newspaper route got me on the road to big business. No one ever forgets their paper-route days, with the freezing weather and the papers flying in bushes. You remember how good you felt when you'd fling a paper and it would land on a front porch perfectly. The paper kids that survive and make the money know you can't keep tossing losers – you get two per customer per year – but otherwise, those papers better hit their mark or it affects your tips, and the whole point any kid is out there is not for the thrill, it's for the cash. So I knew that Ken Woldman had a good aim and could land something sweet on a porch. This meant more to me than the statistics on his businesses that were always climbing up.

I found other things, too. How the Shoe Warehouse went from four stores to four hundred and thirteen in five years by buying up small shoe chains and turning them into Warehouse clones. The *Wall Street Journal* called it "unprecedented growth."

I found out that their stock had started at ten dollars a share and had risen to forty-one dollars. "A searing stock the hot funds love!" proclaimed *Money* magazine.

This guy was golden.

But more than that I knew he wasn't afraid to stick his neck out because he'd been a paper boy and mowed lawns. You're getting to the core of people when you touch their grass and their morning paper.

I made copies of the articles and you could have knocked me over with a pair of peds when a decently cute guy smiled at me right there at the Xerox machine. I smiled back and headed out the door in all my splendour to see what was up with Harry Bender at Gladstone's.

I've never been too good at taking days off.

Twenty

'*C*ARING ABOUT PEOPLE IS THE GREATEST SECRET of success I know.'

Harry Bender was sprinkling Johnson and Johnson Baby Powder on his thick, hairy hands, rubbing them together like a surgeon scrubbing up for an operation. We were standing in the back room of Gladstone's, surrounded by shoe boxes. I'd asked him if he could give me some sales pointers, and I was taking everything in.

'Folks might not like my face or the way I dress or what I'm selling, but they can't deny I care about them.' He looked at me with my sparkling new fashion essence. 'Texas sure seems to be agreeing with you.'

I grinned and followed him onto the floor.

We were off.

And Harry Bender was everywhere, listening . . .

To a woman who had weak ankles.

To a little girl who needed to beat her brother running.

To a man who loved saddle shoes.

'You seen these?' Harry asked, holding up tan calfskins with a brown saddle.

The man's eyes got soft. You can see when it's a passion. Harry just let him stand in the presence of the shoes. Finally the man whispered, 'Twelve medium.' Minutes later he had them on his feet and Harry said quietly, 'My guess is you're not going to be taking them off.'

'You guess right,' the man replied.

Regulars came with their visiting grandchildren, mothers brought babies who were ready for their first pair of shoes, and Harry Bender knew what they wanted. He didn't push. Didn't get frustrated. He could tell when people needed him and when to back away. They could tell he cared the way a class knows a teacher cares about her subject. Too many people try to fake their way through life. That's why the real ones shine so brightly.

When a woman came in apologizing for the battered-up shoes she was wearing, Harry looked at those disgusting things and said, 'Those've been good friends.'

When an older man came in looking sad, Harry said to him, 'How's the world treating you today, my friend?' and that man almost broke down because his wife had died last month and she always came with him to pick out his shoes.

It's the little things, not just in selling, but in life that make the difference. The small moments when you can touch another person. Harry Bender was always looking for them and he found more than any person I'd ever met.

I was walking back to the parking garage when I heard the music. Hand-clapping country music. The kind that makes you want to get up and dance and make a fool of yourself – if, that is, a person was a dancer, which, trust me, I'm not.

I walked towards the sound at the end of the mall. A stage was set up and a band was playing and people in western hats were dancing in a line. I stood on the sidelines to watch, tapping my foot, looking down at my new belt and my green checked skirt, feeling pretty close to perfect.

'All right now,' said one of the musicians on the stage, 'grab a partner for the Texas two-step!'

I folded my arms and leaned against a wall when a male

hand reached out, grabbed my hand, and started leading me to the dance floor. He was really tall and had blonde hair and nice brown eyes and was wearing a big brown cowboy hat.

'Come on,' he said grinning. 'I've been watching you. You need to dance.'

He'd been watching me?

'Uh . . . no . . . I don't dance . . . I . . .'

'Everybody dances in Texas.'

'I'm from Chicago, though, and—'

'Well, you can't help where you're from but you don't have to let it limit you.'

We were on the dance floor now.

'What's your name?' he asked.

'Um . . . Jenna, but . . .'

'Pleased to meet you, Jenna. My name's Will. Now all you have to do is follow me and remember, step, together, step, touch.' He showed me the patterns with his feet.

'I . . . I . . . won't remember this.'

He showed me again. I tried, messed up. He showed me again.

My heart was thumping bad. I knew I was going to blow this and I wanted to sit down. Will took his left hand and grabbed my right one, then he put his right hand around my waist and I realized that Mom had been right. Social dancing skills were always appreciated later in life. I'd never been this close to a younger person of the opposite gender.

I gulped.

The music started.

'Step, together, step, touch,' Will said. I did it, sort of. 'Now just do another step, touch and then repeat.'

I tripped, but he didn't mind and after I got used to being this close to a male I'd never met, after I got used to the steps and going counterclockwise, after my breathing had slowed down, and my face had stopped blushing, I got it.

Step, together, step, touch, step, touch.

'You got it,' Will said, going wide to cover more of the dance floor which I hadn't expected, but I'm here to tell you it was a miracle in the making.

I stayed with him.

I was dancing!

Will was saying how I was a fast study, and I was laughing as we two-stepped around that floor. We danced two dances and I only tripped twice and when his friend came up to us and said they had to go, Will said it had been a pleasure to dance with such a pretty young woman and he wished me well in Chicago. Then he tipped his cowboy hat in a show of respect for my beauty and he and his friend were gone.

I leaned against a store window and watched him go.

Part of me wished he had stayed, but more important than that was the gift he gave me. I looked at myself in the store window and smiled.

Now there, I thought to myself for the first time ever, is a pretty young woman.

Twenty-One

*I*T WAS NINE DAYS TO THE STOCKHOLDERS MEETING, and despite the support from many store managers, the news was bleak. The mail-in ballots were coming in at Gladstone headquarters and Harry Bender's friend, Lyle, said that Elden and the Shoe Warehouse were going to win by a landslide. We'd had an all-out telephoning marathon with me, Harry, Mrs Gladstone and Alice calling all the stockholders and asking them for their support. In one hour seven people hung up on me, two asked if I was crazy, and one said she'd think about it.

I'd just come off the sales floor with Harry Bender, who'd shared with me his two golden sales rules that lifted him from the sewer of despair to the top of his profession.

Rule Number One: Care about people more than what you're selling.

Rule Number Two: Never miss a good opportunity to shut up.

We were sitting in the backroom; Harry Bender was studying a can of Coke like it held some hidden secret to victory.

'It looks pretty bad, doesn't it, Mr Bender?'

He took a long drink, wiped his mouth. 'There isn't any stockholder we talked to who doesn't want to make more money, but there are still lots of folk out there who don't want the Gladstone quality changed. That's the good news. The bad news is we're in the minority.'

'It doesn't sound like anything can be done.'

He slapped his knees. 'This dog fight isn't over yet.' His phone rang. He flipped it open.

'You got Harry . . .'

He listened for a while, then spoke into the receiver: 'Well, that's the worst thing about it, cause the booze doesn't know how to talk to you any other way than lying. So you got to remember that and keep reminding yourself how it was when you were drinking. Feelings get in the way of facts, friend, and you got to distinguish between the two . . . all right then . . . you stay clean. Call back if you need to.'

He folded the phone shut, looked at me.

'Mr Bender, can I talk to you about my dad?'

'Sure thing.'

'I'm getting to the point with him that I'm not sure how to handle things. He hurts me so much when he's around and when he's gone I worry about him and never know if he's coming back. It's like I lose if he's here and lose if he's gone and . . .'

'You told him you feel that way?'

'I couldn't say that to my dad. He doesn't take responsibility for anything, he's just filled with excuses.'

Harry Bender leaned forward. 'Maybe saying it isn't as much for him as it is for you.'

I was about to say he didn't understand when Mrs Gladstone walked in the back.

Harry Bender patted my hand. 'We'll talk about it later. Think about what I said.'

Mrs Gladstone was looking brave, like a politician who knows they've lost an election. 'Is this the wake?' she asked, sarcastically.

'Don't go getting negative on me, old girl.'

'I'm simply being practical, Harry.'

'Shoot, Maddy, any fool can be practical. You want to

start exercising your brain capacity, find some faith and hold onto that.'

Mrs Gladstone laughed. 'I've got faith in you, Harry.'

'Well,' he said smiling, 'let's see what that'll do.'

He patted down his Stetson hat, got out his car keys. 'I've got a meeting with a man who can maybe get us more votes.'

'Who?' Mrs Gladstone demanded.

He smiled mysteriously. 'I haven't got it all clear yet in my head.'

'Harry Bender,' Mrs Gladstone shouted, 'you tell me what you're up to!'

'Not yet,' he said, laughing, and headed out the door.

You know the thing about hope, how it sneaks up behind you when you're sure everything's in the toilet, and starts whispering to you that maybe, just maybe, things could turn around.

That's the gift Harry gave us that night. Some people, all you have to do is stand next to them and you feel protected. Mrs Gladstone said he was always like that, too, a presence of hope, even after all he'd been through, able to laugh darkness in the face.

I wondered if that came from knowing the darkness so well, he'd figured out how to beat it.

Mrs Gladstone said if anyone could bottle and sell Harry Bender, they'd make a fortune. I didn't think any bottle could hold what that man's got.

I pictured him getting out of his Chevy Suburban, saddling up to some millionaire's house, and talking that man over to our side.

I saw him standing up to a podium at the stockholders meeting, giving a speech about truth, justice, and selling shoes, winning the trust of everybody in that room, even Elden, and saving the company.

I saw him telling me that he'd always wanted a daughter like me and that if I didn't mind, he'd be so proud to be my surrogate father and that I could come down and visit him and his wife in Texas any old time I liked.

The stockholders meeting was eight days away. Alice was having dinner with friends and Mrs Gladstone and I were sitting on her beige couch drinking iced tea. I looked at Mrs Gladstone's face. She had deep wrinkles around her mouth, the skin around her eyes was cracked by lines and too much sun – but still, she was beautiful. She smiled from her heart and handed me a big envelope.

'I want to thank you, Jenna, for being so kind to me these weeks. You've made this time downright bearable. Open it.'

I did. Took out a stack of important-looking stiff papers.

'Fifty shares of Gladstone's stock,' she said. 'Worth around twenty-two dollars a share at the moment, but at the end of the week, it should be worth more.'

Twenty-two dollars a share. That was over a thousand dollars. I looked at the papers. Jenna Boller, stockholder.

'Mrs Gladstone . . . wow . . .'

'But you remember, Jenna, business is more than stock, more than profits. Too many people see work as something they've got to do. Floyd and I were lucky, we loved selling shoes, loved meeting the customers, loved trying to do the best we could with what we'd been given. You just can't put a price on that. My father said that God gave people work to help them grow in grace.' She laughed. 'He'd usually tell me that when it was my turn to clean out the chapel.'

The knock on the door woke me from a deep fog. I checked the clock next to my bed – 2:13 AM. I'd fallen asleep with the light on while I was checking the stock market figures in the *Dallas Herald*.

I croaked out, 'Just a minute.'

The knock came louder. I tossed the newspaper aside, knocked over the water glass.

Nice one, Boller.

'I'm coming.'

I blinked hard to find consciousness, half-remembering the dream I was having about me in a solid red Mustang zooming down the highway with a tall, gorgeous college guy at my side. The knock came again. This better be important.

'Jenna!' said Mrs Gladstone from the hall.

I opened the door. Mrs Gladstone stood in her robe, holding it closed close to her throat, crying. Her face was stone grey. Alice stood next to her, crying, too.

'Mrs Gladstone, Alice, are you all right?'

Mrs Gladstone took a faltering step towards me. I reached my hand to help her.

'What is it?'

Her shoulders heaved in sadness. She sat down on the bed, overcome.

She bent over.

Alice cried harder.

'Mrs Gladstone . . .'

'It's Harry Bender,' she said finally, choking back tears. 'He was in a car accident. Hit head-on by a drunk driver.' She shook her old head in disbelief. 'My Lord, Jenna, he's dead.'

Twenty-Two

I SAT AT THE HALVERSTON FUNERAL HOME WITH Mrs Gladstone and Alice in "the viewing room." That's what the snivelling funeral director had called it and I instantly hated him for using that term. He should have said, 'Here's the place where everyone is paying their last respects to Harry Bender, the greatest shoe salesman in the world.' Calling a place like that the viewing room made it sound like we were going to see a movie instead of a person we loved cut down in his prime on a mission of mercy.

I bent over, crying. The tears kept coming and the longer I cried, the longer I needed to keep at it.

I couldn't believe how much you can love a person you've only just met.

I hadn't looked long at the big wooden casket with the flag of Texas draped over it. Sad people were filing past. The men were holding their hats in their hands and the women were dabbing their eyes, but I mostly looked at the leather pumps and western boots slowly moving by. I knew if I looked at the casket with Harry dead and lifeless in it, I would have to leave and I really couldn't handle any of this alone. I needed to stay in this room, surrounded by shoe people.

Mrs Bender looked like she was being held up by sticks. Her face was a mess. The front of her blue dress was wet from sobbing. A man who looked a little like Harry was helping her stand. Every once in a while, someone would just break down loudly and the weeping would fill the room, echoing the loss and sorrow of every person there.

'Lord, have mercy,' a woman cried out, 'struck down by the very people he was trying to save.' Her husband helped her outside.

A man said to a woman that Harry was being buried in his Tony Lama boots that had the lone star of Texas handstitched on the sides, like a cowboy coming home to rest.

Mrs Gladstone sat stiff and small. Alice was all cried out. We sat there for I don't know how long as Harry's friends and family filed by and then another wave of weeping would wash over me as I remembered Harry and all the hope he brought into a room just by breathing.

It was 10:27. I still hadn't gone up to the casket. Mrs Bender left with the man who looked like Harry. Only a few people were left in the room. The funeral director peeked in like he wanted to go home.

'Go,' Mrs Gladstone said to me. 'Say good-bye to your friend.'

I stood up, weak from the tears, walked slowly up the aisle to the dark wooden casket surrounded by flowering cactus trees, saw Harry's head lying there, eyes closed, his cheeks sucked in and all made up, his brown hair too perfect, his mouth sealed shut, it seemed. He looked smaller without the Stetson.

I looked away.

Say good-bye to your friend.

The tears came so hard and from such a deep, ancient place in me, I held onto the casket to steady myself. I was crying big for Harry, sure, but somehow I knew I was crying for all the places in life where dreams die and people get ripped from this earth. I was crying for unfairness and pain and loss and death that comes in so many forms. I was crying for my grandmother who had died to her old self and who would never know that part again, for my father who had lost himself to drinking. I was crying for people who had problems so big they couldn't see them, for myself and Faith and how the father we both needed was so messed up, he could never be who we so hoped he would be. I was crying for my mother and the nightmare she had lived trying to hold things together. I was crying for all the times I felt guilty because my father couldn't stop drinking, which I know wasn't my fault, but the rawness of it, the feelings that I should have been able to help him, but couldn't, burst from me with such stinging, ringing clearness.

I looked down into Harry's dead Texas face. I didn't want to remember him this way. I wanted to remember him booming from the Bass display in the downtown Dallas Gladstone's. I wanted to see him throw back his head and laugh that brave laugh that sends the darkness flying back where it belongs. That's what you should have in the viewing room. A movie of the dead person's life.

I touched the lapel on his dark blue jacket.

I couldn't say anything, so I didn't even try. But if I could have, I would have said, 'I wish I had known you all my life, Harry Bender . . . but I know this . . . I'll never forget you.'

I was in the Cadillac with Mrs Gladstone and Alice, following the funeral procession past the winding gravel road to the back of the Last Roundup Cemetery and Crematorium. Harry Bender's grave was by a little hill overlooking a field of sagebrush. Last night Mrs Bender said the field was going to get turned into a duck pond by next spring, but I think Harry would have preferred sagebrush to duck poop any day. I think he should have been buried somewhere in the mall near the store he loved, but a grave by the ATM machine outside Gladstone's might have killed the festive buying mood and Harry would have hated that.

I'd told myself I wasn't going to cry and I didn't until Mrs Gladstone, Alice and I walked to the freshly dug grave where all the people were gathered. That's when I saw the headstone.

HERE LIES HARRY BENDER – HE GAVE IT HIS BEST SHOD.

It was the ultimate farewell to a true shoe person.

I crossed my arms tight like that would hold me together somehow, and lost it, crying deep and full like I'd lost my dearest friend. I cried for a long time and decided for once in my life not to keep the sadness manageable. It wasn't manageable. It was awful.

The Texas heat was a killer and my tears were mixed with sweat. My face and hands felt sticky. People were crowding in around me. Mrs Gladstone grabbed my hand. Alice bent her head low.

There were only some parts of the funeral I could focus on.

Mrs Bender asked everyone to wear bright colours to celebrate Harry's life. I wore my bright yellow jacket.

Murray Castlebaum had flown in from Chicago and gave a speech about 'the great Mahatma' and all the shoe people put their hands together and bowed down.

A minister said that we don't understand God's ways and that Harry lost his life to the very forces he was fighting against.

A nun said Harry had personally saved hundreds of people from alcoholism and he wasn't going to heaven alone.

Then people were coming up to the grave from the left and right to say something about Harry Bender.

A woman from Shreveport said that if people were just

wearing sandals in heaven, Harry would get them all in leather walkers before they knew what hit them.

A man named Peds Jawarski said he'd personally witnessed Harry's greatest moment in the shoe business, when he'd waited on Imelda Marcos (the wife of the fallen president of the Philippines and a famous shoe lover) who bought thirty-three pairs of shoes from him in two hours. It took two servants to get the boxes in her stretch limo that was parked outside.

A man named Monk Fischer said Harry was such a great salesman, nothing could stop a sale. 'It was the height of flu season,' Monk said, sniffling. 'Harry'd just written up a six-shoe order, but he was looking pretty green around the gills. The woman signed the Visa slip, walked out the store, the last customer of the night, and it wasn't until then that the great man vomited. All over the register, too, but he held that sales slip over his head. Harry would never have puked in the middle of a transaction.'

Mrs Gladstone said there was never a better man, never a more magnanimous employee, and she would be forever grateful to God for calling Harry Bender to sell shoes.

I didn't say anything because I was crying too hard. Murray was sitting next to me on the folding chairs that had been set up.

'You've got something to say, kid, you should say it.'

'I can't.'

'Sure you can.'

Murray gave my elbow a tug and scrunched over so I could get by.

'I don't know these people,' I said to him.

'So?'

I looked around. Elden was sitting behind me, staring at me hard. He was the only one who didn't look sad.

That got me up.

I walked to the front.

Stood by the podium, my legs shaking, the tears coming.

A man was saying how Harry had lent him money when he was down and out. He stepped back from the podium. I walked forward, clutching my Kleenex.

'I only knew Harry Bender for a week,' I said. 'But I loved him like he was my father.' I was crying pretty bad now, but I looked straight at Elden for the next part. 'He knew about selling shoes and what makes business special and how to treat people. He wasn't afraid of saying the truth, wasn't afraid of telling people about the things he'd learned, about the things that almost ruined him. Those were the things that probably became his greatest strength. By talking about them and turning from them, he taught me to not be afraid of the darkness.' I stared at Elden who was staring at me. Everybody from Gladstone's was staring at Elden now.

I used my height. 'So I'm not going to be.'

Elden looked away.

Murray Castlebaum said, 'Amen.'

I squared my shoulders and sat back down. Everyone around me smiled. Mrs Gladstone patted my hand. Alice whispered, 'I never had kids, but I would have wanted a daughter like you, Jenna. No changes.' I held her hand.

A priest who was Harry's friend got up and walked slowly to the casket. He made the sign of the cross, pain and sadness carved across his face, took off the small silver cross he wore around his neck, kissed it, and placed it on the casket.

'Rest well, Harry Bender,' he said softly. 'We've all been made finer for having known you.'

Twenty-Three

*I*T WAS FIVE DAYS AFTER HARRY BENDER'S FUNERAL. The stockholders meeting was tomorrow at three o'clock and there was no way Mrs Gladstone was going to win. It was hard to care about that anymore.

No one knew who Harry had been going to talk to the night he died.

No one knew the plan he was cooking up to get more votes at the meeting.

All his power died with him, it seemed.

Death is a strange thing. Some people die flat out in the midst of something important like Harry, others, like my dad and grandmother, seem to follow a slow path towards it from such different places, taking another step towards dying each day.

I'd been checking the stock market listings every day in the paper because it helped me think about something else. Mrs Gladstone was right – the price of my shares had been climbing, except for Monday, when the market dipped and Gladstone's stock went down a dollar twenty-five per share, which meant I'd lost sixty-two dollars and fifty cents in one day without even getting out of bed. It gained a full two dollars the next day, but I wasn't sure if I had the raw courage it took to be a stockholder.

Mrs Gladstone was angry at Harry's death. She said there was enough unfairness in the world without losing Harry Bender in the prime of his life.

'What did his dying serve?' she shouted.

Alice shook her head and walked off.

I said, 'I don't know, Mrs Gladstone. I just know bad things happen more than I'd like because the world has got more than its share of problems.'

'Well, it's not right!'

'I know it's not, m'am, I—'

She rammed her cane on the floor. 'I don't need platitudes!'

'I didn't mean to—'

'*What?*'

'This is a hard time for everyone, Mrs Gladstone, and—'

'*Enough!*' She stormed from the living room, but it felt like she was still standing there. Anger hangs in places sometimes long after the person is gone. I stomped my foot hard because I had to do something. I hate it when people stop a conversation and I have more to say.

My grandma used to say that some things in life don't have an explanation. What kept her going was believing there was more good in the world than there was bad.

'Sometimes you have to look real hard for it,' she said. 'But I swear to you, Jenna, it's there.'

I promised her I'd look.

And I've been looking ever since.

When my grandmother had to be put in Shady Oaks, she got Gladys as her roommate.

When Mom started the nightshift, she got time and a half pay.

When Dad came back to town, I was pushed out the door to Texas and got to know Mrs Gladstone and met Harry Bender and Alice.

You never know where the road's going to take you. I think sometimes it's less important that you get to your destination than the sidetrips you take along the way.

I walked down the hall to Mrs Gladstone's room and knocked on the door.

'*What?*' she shouted.

'I'm going to make a grilled cheese sandwich, Mrs Gladstone, and wondered if you wanted one.'

Silence.

'I make the best grilled cheese sandwich in the world,' I added humbly.

The door opened. She was standing there in camel slacks and a cream-coloured shirt. 'I haven't had a grilled cheese in years.'

'This is your lucky day,' I said and headed towards the kitchen.

I stood at the long tiled kitchen counter, brushing olive oil on thick oatmeal bread; I spread the other side with honey mustard, layered on cheddar cheese, tomato slices, and sautéed Canadian bacon, placed a slice of oatmeal bread on top, put the two sandwiches in a cast-iron skillet sizzling with butter. Mrs Gladstone leaned against the opposite wall, watching me. Never miss a good opportunity to shut up, Harry Bender had said. I kept quiet, flipped the sandwiches when they got perfectly browned on one side as Mrs Gladstone cleared her old voice. We were standing there, as different as two human beings on this earth could be, and yet we were connected.

I put the sandwiches on two plates, cut them at an angle to show off, put them on the round glass kitchen table by the window that overlooked the rock garden. Our kitchen table at home overlooked the fire escape.

Mrs Gladstone came to the table slowly. She'd been moving slower since Harry Bender died. We all had. Grieving sucks energy from a person's core. She took a bite of the sandwich; her face lit up.

'Superb.'

I tried mine. It was, too.

She said, 'If Harry were alive, Jenna, what do you think he'd be doing right now?'

I checked my watch. Four-thirteen. Wednesday. 'He'd be selling shoes, Mrs Gladstone, doing his level best to make you rich right up until the store closed.'

She laughed.

'And he wouldn't be giving up. He'd be talking to people, thinking about what he was going to say at the stockholders meeting. I think being in AA for as long as he was, he got used to seeing all kinds of problems turn around and that gave him courage.'

Mrs Gladstone ate the last bite of her sandwich. 'I'm about to lose my company, but I certainly am well fed.'

I put my sandwich down. 'Mrs Gladstone, I don't think you realize how strong you are.'

She looked at me irritated, but I couldn't stop.

'I know your hip hurts and you've got that operation coming up – I mean your strength as a person. I know what it's like to be tossed aside by an important person, Mrs Gladstone. It makes you think you're not worth fighting for, that people can do whatever they like and you don't fight back or tell them how you're feeling. You just keep being a good sport, hoping the person will change, while people walk all over you. I let my dad do that. I just took it like I was powerless, like I didn't have a right to be angry and say no.'

'And do you really think telling him would have changed anything, Jenna?'

'Probably not. I don't know. But I think speaking the truth would have changed me.' I was standing now, waving my napkin. 'Because I'm angry, Mrs Gladstone! I've been afraid of it for so long. Afraid that if I let him know how I felt, he'd hate me, like I was supposed to be perfect and make up for the fact that he had all these problems!'

Mrs Gladstone was studying her plate like the answer was in the blue and white flowered pattern. 'I'm angry, too,' she said quietly.

'Then go to that meeting tomorrow and kick some butt, ma'am. That's what we're in Texas for, isn't it?'

She stared at the plate. 'I don't know anymore . . .'

'And wave the cane around, Mrs Gladstone. That cane's a real killer.'

Twenty-Four

W^{*HACK.*}

W   The killer cane came down on the banister.

Mrs Gladstone announced, 'I'd rather eat live snakes than go to this meeting!'

It was three-thirty – Thursday. The stockholders meeting started in one and a half hours. I was standing in Mrs Gladstone's kitchen, wearing my green shirt, khaki skirt, and 1½-inch-heeled pumps. Mrs Gladstone stuck a bony thumb towards the door, which meant we were leaving now or else.

We walked out the door. Alice was waiting for us on the porch. The heat was mean and heavy. I'd washed the Cadillac myself early this morning, but nobody noticed. Mrs Gladstone said, 'Let's get this over with.'

Alice put her hand around Mrs Gladstone's shoulder, but Mrs Gladstone shook it off. I helped her in the backseat. She was wearing a red two-piece suit with a striped blouse, and sat there trying to be tough, writing notes in her blue leather folder with angry movements.

Alice said, 'Madeline, honey . . .' and got glared at.

I started up the Cadillac. 'You sure look ready for anything, Mrs Gladstone,' I said and headed down the driveway as she grunted. It wasn't until I took a quick peek at her in the rearview mirror that I saw her smile.

I pulled up to the tall glass headquarters of Gladstone's

Shoes in downtown Dallas. The windows were sparkling like they had no idea the deceit that was going on behind them. The sun was shining like all was well. The parking lot was filling up with Mercedes and Chevy Suburbans. I dropped Mrs Gladstone and Alice off at the entrance and said I'd meet them inside.

Mrs Gladstone moved slowly to the glass double doors, looked back at me and smiled bravely. Then she squared her old shoulders and walked inside with Alice behind her.

I parked in the Executive Only section and if anyone gave me any guff about it, I was going to give it right back. I cracked my knuckles and got out of the car.

The heat hung thick and depressive like a rotten mood. I walked in the building, followed the signs to the stockholders meeting, down the long, polished hall. A large, jovial man was standing at the door to the meeting room, checking off people's names as they came in. I jingled the car keys in my hand and started toward him.

That's when Elden Gladstone jumped in front of me.

'Jenna,' he said, 'I want to thank you personally for *all* you've done for my mother.'

You could have knocked me over. I looked down at him.

Then he swiped the car keys from my hand, put them in his pocket. 'But we're not going to be needing your services now that she is retiring.'

My heart was beating very fast.

'You understand,' Elden said smoothly. 'We'll have someone drive you to the airport.'

This wasn't happening.

'I'm sorry, sir, I don't understand. I'm supposed to drive your mother back to Chicago.'

Elden broke into a fake smile. 'Let's put it another way. 'You're *fired*.'

I stepped back.

'You will be on the seven PM flight today back to Chicago. Here's your ticket.' He slapped it in my hand. 'Your severance cheque will be mailed to you at home along with your luggage. Don't expect a referral from this company. *Ever.*'

I stood there holding the ticket, frozen.

A tall man with a bushy moustache appeared like a bad dream. Elden said, 'Mac will get you a taxi. *No one* pushes me around.' Then he laughed and started walking off.

'I'd like to talk to your mother, Mr Gladstone. She's the one who hired me.' I said this with more courage than I felt.

Elden Gladstone turned to me like just looking at me hurt his eyes. 'My mother doesn't have anything to do with this company anymore,' he snapped.

'She wanted me at that meeting, sir.'

He looked at my shoes. 'Stockholders only.'

'But . . .'

He nodded to Mac, who took my arm firmly and led me out the door, onto the stifling street. I tried to shake my arm free; I couldn't do it. My insides were shaking.

A cab pulled up, Mac gave the driver thirty dollars.

'Dallas Airport,' Mac said coarsely to the driver, and opened the door for me. I got inside because I didn't know what else to do.

Think.

'Any bags?' the driver asked.

'They'll be sent,' Mac said flatly.

I felt like I was getting kicked out of the country.

Mac stood firm by the cab in case I made a break for it. He crossed his thick arms and glared at me.

I looked away. I couldn't think.

'Dallas Airport it is,' said the cabbie and started off.

Twenty-Five

DEFEATED TEEN DEPARTS DALLAS.
    The cabdriver moved in and out of traffic like a man on a mission. He was wearing a Dallas Cowboys hat, talking about how the Cowboys were the winningest team in football history. Ask me if I care.

'Where you headed, miss?'

I didn't answer. I wasn't sure.

'Where's home?' he tried again.

I sat there frozen.

Mrs Gladstone had hired me.

Mrs Gladstone needed me.

'You OK back there?'

'Can you stop?' I asked him.

He pulled to the side of the road.

'I just got fired.'

'Tough break.'

'It shouldn't have happened.'

The driver turned to look at me. 'You make somebody nervous or what?'

I looked up. 'I guess I did.'

He nodded. 'My brother used to say you can't make nobody nervous unless they got something to hide.'

That cleared my mind. 'Will you turn around, sir?'

'You want to go back?'

'Yes.'

'You sure?'

Was I?

'I've got something to finish,' I said.

'Hold on, miss.' The cabbie did a three-point turn, nearly sideswiping a potato chip truck, and headed back to Gladstone's headquarters. 'Those big shots in suits, they think they can push anybody around. I pick 'em up, drive 'em to the airport, they act like I don't exist.' He pulled into the driveway. 'You want the front or the back?'

'I don't want anybody to see me.'

'You want the back.'

The cabbie drove around the back and stopped at a smaller door. I told him to keep the money.

He smiled at me. 'Those guys breathe the same oxygen as anybody else. Remember that.'

It seemed like a good idea at the time. The problem was the back door was locked.

It was 5:15. The meeting had already started.

How could I get in?

The Texas sun cast a long shadow of my figure. Grandma always said there was nothing more commanding than a tall woman who used her height. Height was about all I had left. I walked tall to the front of the building, through the front door, past a medium-sized bored security guard.

'ID please,' he said.

I had one of those. Whipped it out, looked down at him like if he tried something funny, he'd be sorry.

'I'm late for a meeting,' I said brusquely.

'OK, OK.' He waved me forward.

Perception is everything.

Took the escalator up past waterfalls, flowering cactus trees, shiny mirrored walls that showed my tallness off at every imaginable angle. Took a Texas-sized breath. Don't panic now. Saw the sign pointing to the meeting room. Walked to it quickly.

Locked.

I could hear the din of voices inside. I ran to the side door – locked, too. I raced down the hallway of Gladstone's corporate headquarters, my $1\frac{1}{2}$ inch heels clicking on the floor tile, and ran smack into a grey-haired man with a briefcase, almost knocking him down.

'I'm sorry, sir.'

He pointed to the closed door. 'That one locked, too?' He had a deep Texas voice.

I nodded.

'Well,' he said, 'there's always knocking.' The man strode to the big wooden double doors and gave them a strong *rat-a-tat*.

Instantly another man in a grey suit opened the door.

'Looks like we're late,' the man I almost knocked down said.

'Come on in.'

The gatekeeper motioned us inside. Elden was sitting on a platform, listening to a woman with a bun read minutes from the last meeting. He froze solid when he saw me.

'I hate these things,' the man I almost knocked down whispered to me.

'This is my first one. I'm pretty excited about voting my shares.'

'Good to take an interest in your investments.'

Elden was shooting daggers at me from the stage. He caught Mac's eye who looked shocked and started walking towards me. I thought about asking the man I almost knocked down if he wouldn't mind being a human shield just for this meeting. He was big enough – six three at least. Just stand in front of me, sir . . .

Mac stood at the end of my aisle and motioned me towards him.

I shook my head.

The woman reading the minutes of the last meeting was droning on and on about how many people were present and how many employees Gladstone's had nationally.

Mac made an emphatic gesture that said I was to obey *now*.

I looked away.

'I think that fella is trying to get your attention,' the man I almost knocked down said.

'Actually, sir, he's trying to kick me out. I got fired today. I'm Mrs Gladstone's assistant.'

He took off his glasses and looked at me.

'They tried to send me back to Chicago without my luggage,' I whispered. 'But I'm going to vote my fifty shares in this meeting even though I'm scared to do it.'

Mac started pushing past seated people to get to me. He stood angrily by the man I almost knocked down and whispered, 'Stockholders only.'

'She is a stockholder,' said the man.

'Fifty shares worth,' I whispered to Mac whose face got red. 'Mrs Gladstone gave them to me and I'm going to vote them. And I'm not too happy about that dip in profits on Monday.'

The man I almost knocked down stifled a laugh.

Mac tried to push past him, but he held out his big arm to hold Mac back. 'I think that's enough,' the man said quietly to Mac, and I absolutely agreed.

'I let the cab driver keep your money,' I added. 'And I'd rather pack my own suitcases, too. You know how it is.'

Mac backed off and stood razor straight by the locked door. Elden was steaming on the podium like a bad radiator. He glared at Mac. Mac shrugged at him. Ken Woldman was sitting next to Elden, just grinning away. You could almost hear the calculator going off in his head tallying how much money he was going to make with this new deal.

I looked towards the podium because Mrs Gladstone had just been introduced. She walked towards the microphone with absolute elegance. I sat extra tall so she'd see me. She looked at the microphone like it was crawling with bugs.

'Not everyone gets to be present at their own funeral,' she said, looking out at the crowd, looking into the faces of the people, not running or hiding, just being brave.

Alice was up front. The shoe people leaned forward, the other ones leaned back.

'My son tells me that the days of Gladstone's Shoes are over as we knew them,' she said crisply. 'He tells me that price cutting and warehousing are the new world order of this new retail world. I must tell you truthfully, I don't know how to do business in this new environment. I only know how to sell one good pair of shoes at a time.

'My father, many of you know, was a Baptist minister. You can't live in a house with a preacher and not have some of it rub off.'

People were smiling.

'I'd like to tell you a story I heard him tell over the years about a man who owned a big construction company and wanted to build the best house that money could buy. He put his son in charge of the building, since his son was his partner in business and he trusted him. Every week the man asked the son, "Are you building it well, son? Are you using the best material, the best builders?" And every week the son answered, "Yes, Father. I haven't skimped anywhere." But the truth was the son had cut corners in materials and workmanship and was pocketing the money. And when the house was finally built, the father asked him one last time, "Did you build it well, son, with the finest of everything?" Again the son said he had. And then the father, busting with joy, said, "Then I give it to you, son. It's your home to live in. I wanted to give you the best I knew how to give.'"

Quiet hung in the room.

'And so,' Mrs Gladstone concluded, 'I am retiring today; officially, unequivocally, after fifty years of building and growing and aching and celebrating with this company. I leave you with the words of my late husband, I commend them to my son and to every person involved in this company and beyond: if the time ever comes when you can no longer look the customer in the eye, then it is time to get out of the business. I am taking his advice. I am getting out now.'

There was an audible gasp as Mrs Gladstone turned slowly like a great queen and sat down.

I jumped up. 'Mrs Gladstone, *no!*'

People didn't know what to do. A few clapped. Most just sat there, their mouths hanging open like dead fish. Elden lunged towards the podium and said something mangy about his mother's great contributions to the shoe industry and her charisma as a leader, but who he really was spoke so loudly, his fake words were drowned out in a cloud of bull. Then Ken Woldman tried to convince Mrs Gladstone that her company would be safe under his care, he guaranteed it. Then other people got up and started talking and saying how everyone wanted the stock to go up and Gladstone's would be made stronger by this merger and the company was going full steam ahead.

If Harry Bender was alive, he would have done something.

'You got something to say, kid,' Murray Castlebaum would have said if he'd been here, 'you should say it.'

So I started walking.

I didn't know why.

Didn't know what I was going to say.

Squeezed past the man I almost knocked down, past

other stockholders' knees and feet, past Mac the bouncer, who was cracking his knuckles like tough guys do right before they're going to beat someone up. He grabbed my arm tight, but I ground my 1½ inch heel into his foot and he let go fast. I started towards the aisle, walking tall, looking Elden straight in his angry face because when you've already been fired, what else are they going to do to you?

Elden whispered something to his mother who said loudly, 'Oh, but she is a stockholder, Elden. Fifty shares. I gave them to her.' Mrs Gladstone saw me walking up the aisle and her face lit up like Chicago's Michigan Avenue at Christmas. I walked up the stairs of the platform, grabbed Mrs Gladstone's welcoming hand, pushed past Elden, stood in front of Ken Woldman, said, 'How do you do, sir, I had a paper route, too.' I walked to the podium like I had one free throw left before the whistle.

I really hate public speaking.

I looked at the microphone and aimed.

'I got fired today,' I said as the crowd gasped. 'I'm Mrs Gladstone's driver and assistant and Mr Gladstone tried to put me on a plane back to Chicago because I didn't like the way he's been treating his mother. I don't like the way he's been treating this company, either.'

Elden started towards me, 'I think that's enough!'

The man I almost knocked down bolted from his chair and shouted, 'Let her speak!'

Yield, rat boy!

Elden sat down, blistering.

I took a huge breath, gripped the podium. 'See, I know what selling shoes ought to be because I had the privilege to know Harry Bender. I also work with Murray Castlebaum in Chicago and I've been hanging with Mrs Gladstone all summer. I've gotten dunked in what good business should be like so much so that I can smell something wrong a mile off.'

Mac was steaming.

I could hear Elden behind me making rodent noises.

'I've been on the road with Mrs Gladstone this summer. We've visited Gladstone stores from Peoria to Shreveport. And I can tell you those economy brands aren't doing this company one bit of good. People come into a Gladstone's expecting quality, just like people on a paper route expect the carrier to deliver the paper they ordered. You don't start tossing a *Chicago Weekly* on the porch if your customer wants a *Chicago Tribune*. You won't have any chance of keeping that business.' I turned to face Ken Woldman. 'Will you, Mr Woldman?'

'No,' he said quietly, 'you won't.'

Keep talking, Boller.

I looked back at the crowd. 'I understand we need profits to keep business going. I understand we need marketing to make sure companies do well. But I don't understand why you have to sacrifice quality and good feeling with that. The people Harry Bender sold shoes to came back to him again and again, they brought their children to him, and their grandchildren to him not because Gladstone's is the only shoe store in Texas but because they trusted him to do the right thing by them.'

'I'm the youngest person in this room by far, but I can tell you that the teenagers I know take their money seriously. We work hard for it just like all of you. We're looking for products to buy that we can trust. We're looking for respect when we walk into a store. I think one of the best ways to show respect to anyone is to give them the best you've got to give. I can't believe that what Gladstone's has offered to customers all these years is now old fashioned.' I turned to Ken Woldman and saw that he was smiling at me. So I took a chance and tried to land one sweet on the porch. 'So I'm taking my fifty shares of stock and I'm voting that Mrs Gladstone stay with this company somehow. I know that's not on the ballot, but that's what I'm going to write on mine. Because I know that if she stays connected, this company will have a chance to keep the good things that everyone expects from Gladstone's Shoes that people like Mrs Gladstone and Murray Castlebaum and Harry Bender always kept safe.'

I looked out at everyone who was looking back at me and swallowed so hard I almost choked.

'I'm done,' I said.

The man I almost knocked down was waving his hat in the back. 'I'm voting with you!' And several other people shouted that they were, too.

Then more said they would and I turned around to look at Mrs Gladstone who was grinning. Elden was darting back and forth like a rat who'd just been caged.

TEEN 1

VERMIN 0

I strutted off the stage.

The man I almost knocked down said that Harry Bender had been to his house the night he died, having sold him, a large, independent stockholder, on the value of Gladstone's all over again. I smiled big because if anybody could keep selling after he died, it was Harry. Soon over half the people in the room were applauding.

But the majority has it.

We filled in our ballots, sent them forward, and waited. Ken Woldman shook my hand, paper person to paper person, then he went over to talk to Mrs Gladstone. They huddled together for the longest time while Elden groaned. I heard Alice say, 'I did her hair, you know.'

Then the secretary with the tight grey bun, who looked like she hated the world, walked to the podiuim, holding a piece of paper.

'The sale has been approved by the holders of seventy-three per cent of the voting shares,' she announced.

It was so hard to hear the official words.

Mrs Gladstone stood straight and proud on the podium like the true person she was.

Elden shook Ken Woldman's hand gleefully.

'But,' the woman continued, 'over four hundred voters have written in requesting that Madeline Gladstone stay with the new company.'

People were applauding and Ken Woldman took the microphone and said to the crowd, 'Now I'm a numbers man, and I know the numbers don't lie. There's room in this company for both kinds of shoe stores. Madeline and I have been having a real interesting talk and I'd like to keep her on as a member of the board of directors and give her complete charge of quality control. I need to learn what this woman knows about selling shoes.'

Elden jumped up and said maybe they should talk about this in private before making big decisions, but his voice got drowned out by more clapping. Mrs Gladstone clomped up to the podium, raised that wicked cane of hers, and said, '*Complete* charge, Ken?'

Ken Woldman held out his tanned, prosperous hand. 'Yes, ma'am. That's what I said.'

She rammed that cane on the floor, shook his hand neat, and said, 'I accept. And my son can tell you that the women in my family live to a ripe, ornery old age.' She turned to Elden. 'So, Elden, I'm going to be around for a long, long time. Won't that be nice, dear?'

Elden half-smiled because the whole world was watching and slumped in his chair, soleless.

Twenty-Six

I STEERED THE CADILLAC ONTO I 20 EAST AND watched the last of Dallas disappear in my rearview mirror.

It was so hard to leave, but like my grandmother always said, wherever we go, we take everything we've ever learned with us.

Alice was staying in Dallas to visit with friends and gloat. She told me how to keep my bangs wispy and that my hair needed to be cut like clockwork every six weeks or everything she'd done for me would go out the window. She flounced out my shirt and told me to always keep my belt buckle shined. I hugged her for a long time and then she said, 'Oh, we'll see each other again, honey. I'm not through changing your life yet.'

We didn't stop much along the way. Mrs Gladstone had to get to work putting traps down around Gladstone's to catch the rodents that were sure to crawl in through the pipes. She said that she was going to need to be coming back and forth to Texas after her operation to kick butt and she'd sure like me, her assistant, to be driving her if we could coordinate trips with my school vacations.

When we caught sight of the Chicago skyline, it just took my breath away. There isn't a better skyline anywhere with the old and the new combined, with the vision of the architects so proudly maintained. I mentioned that the same thing could happen at Gladstone's Shoes, combining the old with the new, and Mrs Gladstone said she wasn't *that* old, and I lied and said of course not, and tried to change the subject.

Mom and Faith were waiting for me when we pulled onto Astor Street and they hardly recognized me with my new haircut and adult persona.

'Your daughter,' Mrs Gladstone said to Mom, 'is an extraordinary young woman. It has been an honour to be with her this summer.'

Mom's lower lip started going and she said she knew and I stood tall like the assistant to the Director for Quality Control and didn't cry even though I wanted to.

I pulled the Cadillac into the garage with everyone looking and didn't lurch or lunge once. We all helped Mrs Gladstone with her bags and she said she'd see me Monday morning for brainstorming.

'Yes, ma'am. You want me to pick you up?'

'Well, of course I do.'

'Sorry.'

Mrs Gladstone got strict when she was feeling emotional.

We spent days catching up.

Faith told me how she visited Grandma every Tuesday when I was gone. She even wrote down what happened at each visit so she wouldn't forget to tell me and showed me her notes. Little sisters do have their moments. She said that Grandma called her Jenna twice and once Grandma remembered her name.

'I didn't do it as well as you, Jenna, but—'

'You did great, Faith.'

'I did better with Grandma than I did with Dad.'

Dad started calling the house drunk late at night a week after I left. Faith was home alone.

'I couldn't understand him half the time, Jenna. I

wanted to talk to him, tell him what I was doing, but . . .'

'You can't talk to him when he's drunk.'

'We got the unlisted number and the calls stopped.' Faith's eyes got sad. 'I never knew what you had to go through, Jenna. I never understood how you protected me.'

I shrugged and said it was no big deal.

'It's a big deal,' Faith assured me.

Mom got a raise and a new boyfriend while I was gone. The raise didn't take any getting used to; the boyfriend did, even though Mom assured me, 'We're taking it *very, very* slow.' Not that I didn't like Evan right off – he didn't try to win me over like some men do. He was funny and knew all about computers. I'd just expected Mom and Faith to be exactly the same when I got back – no changes. I knew this wasn't fair because of how I'd changed. We'd all been on journeys this summer.

I was walking through Lincoln Park, my favourite thinking place, past the South Pond with the paddleboats and duck feeders. I walked up Dickens to Clark Street, heading to Opal's house, when my father pulled up beside me in a little grey Saturn.

How did he find me?

He motioned me inside the car.

I wasn't ready for this.

'OK, Dad.'

I got in. It wasn't until he started down Clark Street that I realized he'd been drinking.

'Dad, stop.'

He shook his head like he was trying to clear it, grabbed the wheel tighter, veered the car away from a bicyclist.

'Dad!'

'I'm OK, Jenna girl.' He kept going, swerving.

'You're not OK! Stop the car!'

He didn't.

He turned right on Armitage, tyres squeaking, almost rammed into a stop sign.

'Dad, you're drunk! Stop the car!'

'I'm driving here, Jenna girl!'

'No! You're not driving anymore!'

'Whose gon stop me?'

'I'm not going to be road kill! Do you hear me? I said, do you hear me?'

I tried to take the wheel from him, but he pushed me away. How do I stop the car?

I looked madly around.

Couldn't reach the brakes.

Couldn't take the keys out.

Think.

I shoved the gear shift into neutral, pulled like crazy on the hand brake between us.

Work!

'Hey!' Dad shouted as the car went slower, slower, then finally stopped just short of hitting a parked van.

'No more, Dad!'

A policewoman got out of a patrol car, ran towards us.

I pushed the door open, jumped out. 'This is the hardest thing I've ever had to do,' I shouted. 'This man is my father. He's been driving drunk.'

'What're you doing?' Dad bellowed.

'Step out of the car, sir,' said the officer.

Dad did, not well.

'Sir, have you been drinking?'

Dad looked down, swayed a little. 'Nah.'

She gave him the alcohol balloon test; Dad reeled in front of the little white balloon, finally blew it up. In seconds, my father became an official drunk driver.

'Sir, I'm going to have to bring you in.'

'Ahhhh . . .' Dad shook his head, looked through me like I wasn't there, and was led off.

'It could have been you who killed him, Dad! It could have been you!'

I ran home, pumping my long legs, stretching faster and faster on each block. I took the stairs to our apartment two at a time, and crashed against the front door.

'I'm OK.'

I said this as much for myself as for my mother as I ran past her and Evan. They were sitting at the dining room table eating Brie and oatmeal crackers, gazing into each other's eyes.

'Jenna?' Mom got up and started after me. She was in her white nurse pantsuit with her name tag: 'Carol Boller, RN.' Her hair was extra curly because of the humidity.

I held up my hands. 'I'm fine.'

'You're not.'

If you both watch closely you can see me fall apart.

Ready?

I ran through the kitchen.

Ran past Faith, who was making an egg-salad sandwich.

Ran into the bathroom that Faith and I shared, locked the old, scratched door with the bent copper key, kicked aside the hair dryer on the floor, turned on the shower full blast.

I shook off my stacked leather shoes, threw off my clothes, pushed back the ornamental fish shower curtain, and climbed in.

I threw back my aching head as the water pulsated over me.

I hated him.

Terrified Teen Has Drunk Father Arrested.

I closed my eyes, stuck my face directly under the warm spray.

Just wash it off me.

I saw in my mind Dad staggering home when I was small.

Sitting there in his white bathrobe, hungover, when I'd come home from school.

I never wanted friends to come home with me.

Daddy's sick, that's what we'd say.

The water pounded my eyes, face, neck. I washed myself three times. I remembered when I cut my foot and was in the hospital getting stitches. Everything is scary when you're six. Dad walked in holding the biggest stuffed elephant in the world.

I slammed the memory blinds shut.

Let the water do its work.

Clean Teen Faces World – Vows to Fight On.

I turned off the shower, thankful for the fog that had settled on the mirror, which meant I didn't have to see myself. The towels were heavy with wetness, I dried myself as best I could, put on my yellow terry cloth robe. A knock rapped on the door.

'Jenna?' It was my mother.

I unlocked the bathroom door to her worried face.

'Evan's gone,' she said.

Mom hadn't had a boyfriend in a long time.

'Did he leave because of me?'

'He left because it was the right thing to do.' Mom planted her emergency room nurse shoes in front of me like she did when she had to give a patient a shot who didn't want one.

'Tell me,' she said.

I leaned against the door; told her. I didn't cry.

Mom pushed her own angry tears away.

Don't cry, Mom. I know how much you hate him.

She went into ER nurse mode, sitting me down, getting me water.

Was I all right?

—— 161 ——

Yes.

Hurt in any way?

No.

Did I want her to stay home tonight, not go into work? She'd be happy to—

No.

We sat on the wobbly wooden stools as night fell on the kitchen – mother and daughter trying to reach each other, but more than anything just swallowing the pain.

Twenty-Seven

I BOUGHT MY CAR THE NEXT WEEK – A CHEVY Cavalier with a sun roof and torn bucket seats. It wasn't quite the one I'd dreamed of – I couldn't afford the Corvette convertible – but it was red, and most importantly, it was mine. Opal came with me when I drove it off the lot. She christened it with sparkling apple cider – opened the bottle and poured it over the left front bumper as the used car salesman applauded.

A red car. My dad would approve. He'd gotten out of jail when Sueann Turnbolt paid his bail. I knew this because I'd called the jail. I'd had the car for three days and already I'd waxed it twice. I used the gentle circling motion Dad taught me when he used to wax his cars, careful to not leave any streaks or buildup. It's funny the things we hold onto from our parents and the things we leave behind.

I was driving down Lake Shore Drive with the picnic in a basket – fried chicken, olive rolls, fruit salad, and lemon cookies. I pulled into the driveway of Shady Oaks Nursing Home and walked inside, up the stairs, past the nurses station, past the tired, blank stares of the old people in wheelchairs and walkers to my grandmother's room. Gladys was sitting in a chair by the window reading. She smiled so big when I walked in.

'Well,' she declared, 'look, Millie, it's Jenna. Back from Texas.'

'Texas,' my grandmother said flatly.

I handed Gladys a postcard of the big Texas sky. 'That piece of the sky I promised you.'

Gladys held it to her heart, smiling.

'Come on, Grandma,' I said, 'we're going on that picnic.'

Grandma looked at Gladys, who said, 'Millie, you go on now with Jenna. She'll take good care of you.'

Grandma wanted to wear her pink sweater even though I told her it was hot. I helped her on with it. The memory board had my daisy postcard pinned to it alongside one of Faith's new modelling photos. I took off my little sign that read 'Jenna's gone to Texas. She'll see you when she gets back.'

I pointed to Faith's smiling face. 'Faith and I are going to come together next week to see you Grandma, but I wanted to spend some time with you alone.'

Grandma walked out the door with me like a little child. It took a few tries to get her in the car, but once we got moving, she started smiling.

'I know you don't remember everything like you wished,' I said as I pulled onto Lake Shore Drive, 'but I promised you when I got my car I'd take you on a picnic.'

'Picnic,' said my grandmother.

I drove to the Belmont Harbour exit, got off by the boats, parked near the water, and helped my grandmother out of the car. She walked with me slowly. I found a park bench, put a blanket down. Her face lit up for a minute.

'Jenna?' she said.

I smiled. She remembered. 'Yeah, Grandma, it's me.'

'You never liked keeping your underpants on,' she announced.

I laughed. 'That's not true!'

'You were always running buck naked around the yard.'

I opened the picnic basket, laughing. Of all the things about me to remember. 'I got over it,' I said and handed her a plate.

'I don't remember things like I used to,' she said sadly.

'I know.'

'I can see you as a child sometimes, but not . . .'

'I know.'

'I would like to remember you more,' she said, looking off as a pigeon swooped down and ate a piece off her cookie.

'I know. It's not your fault.'

She ate a little bit and didn't say much; she fed the squirrels, though.

So I talked.

About shoes and Harry Bender.

About Mrs Gladstone and Cadillacs.

About driving and earning money and buying my car and what happens to a person when they've been to Texas.

'I think Texas makes you think about things in a bigger way' I said. 'I've never been anywhere that changed me so much.'

Grandma was picking at her shoelaces.

'Tight,' she said.

I bent down to check them, loosened the laces, made sure the tongues lay flat; relaced them. She was silent as I helped.

The grass was scorched and brown from the hot summer sun. We headed towards the car, Grandma and me.

I said, 'I remember when I was a little girl and we'd make that grape jam from the grapes in your yard and I'd get it all over everything . . .'

'Including the cat,' she said softly.

I opened the car door. She got inside and grabbed my hand like it was a life raft. I crouched down, held her hand for the longest time.

So much sadness.

So much pain.

But remembering the good things – that's what keeps anyone going.

Twenty-Eight

I SAT ON THE ROCK IN THE ROOKERY OF THE Lincoln Park Zoo waiting for my father. I always liked the Rookery because it ws a little haven tucked away from the noise of the city. It had a small pond and rocks and moss and plants surrounding it. Ducks swam and birds sang and butterflies fluttered overhead. I always felt at peace here, even if things were going wrong other places.

A mother duck and her babies swam by. Funny, how in nature you see so many single female parents. Lions, bears, dogs, cats. The mother always gets the kids, the father goes off somewhere to start another litter. I mentioned this to my mother once. She said anyone who gets the kids gets the deal.

I threw a piece of bread into the water. The mother duck let the lead baby get it. Then another piece of bread hit the water; it wasn't mine. I turned to look.

My father was standing there holding a bag of bread.

'I didn't know if you'd come,' I said.

He threw another hunk of bread into the pool. 'I didn't either.'

I tried not to study him to see if he was drunk. He looked OK, but . . .

'I'm not drunk,' he said, sounding normal.

'OK.'

'You wanted to talk.'

'Yeah.'

Dad sat down on the rock that was higher than mine. He was wearing clean jeans and a golf shirt.

'I don't apologize for what happened with your licence,' I started.

He let out a long sigh.

'I would do it again, Dad, to save your life . . . and mine. I had a good friend who—'

'I was handling it, Jenna.'

'*No.*' This was going down the toilet fast.

'I lost my licence, Jenna! I've got to do six weeks of community service!'

Good.

'Just listen,' I pleaded.

I threw up my hands and the words poured out of me.

'I remember the smells mostly, Dad – the drinks with the half-eaten olives – the aroma of my childhood was gin, bourbon, and scotch. I'd sniff the glasses in the house; took a lick off a bottle once. It was awful. Something's wrong with us, I kept thinking. This doesn't happen at my friends' houses.

'I'd go to liquor stores with you, Dad – all the store owners knew you. You were happy in those shops and I tried to be happy, too, but I knew that in just a few hours things were going to change.

'After the divorce I used to sit on your side of the bed and pretend you were still there. I'd wrap myself up in the bathrobe you left behind and curl up like you were going to drop through the ceiling all healed. I'd look for you around every corner. I'd try so hard to be perfect so you'd come back. I tried to protect everyone – help Faith, be no problem to Mom. I thought if things were easier you might stop drinking.'

I slapped the rock, shaking. 'I took your drinking on my shoulders, Dad! But I can't keep it there anymore. *I've changed.* I love you, but I can't be with you unless *you* change because seeing you so out of control, seeing you wasting your life is too hard for me. I can't pretend like you don't have a problem. You need help, Dad! You're an alcoholic. There's help everywhere for what you've got. But you've got to want to get it.'

'*I know,*' he hissed, '*how to handle my liquor.*'

'No,' I said back to him. 'That's a lie. You don't.'

He got up slowly, glared at his bag of bread, and hurled the whole thing into the pond, scaring the ducks that scattered quacking in every direction.

I stood up, too – stood tall. 'Please hear me, Dad. If you keep drinking I won't see you, I won't talk to you on the phone. I need a sober father. Faith does too.'

'That's pretty rough, Jenna.'

'I know it.'

Dad walked heavily across the stepping stones towards the gate, then turned back to look at me – anger, hurt, and love carved on his face.

I looked at him, too, but not the old way with guilt and fear. I didn't know what would happen now, later, or ever. All I knew is that I'd said it finally – spoke the truth – and saying it was like losing five hundred miserable pounds that I'd been lugging around for most of my life.

He stood there for the longest time, then shrugged finally and headed out. It wasn't until then that I realized I'd been crying.

I always wondered why I had a father who was an alcoholic.

Now I knew.

It made me strong.

It made me different.

It showed me how to say no to the darkness.

I looked at the pond. A few ducks were back swimming round Dad's plastic bag.

It wasn't right, throwing that bag in there. This was a bird sanctuary.

I found a long stick and fished it out of the pond. 'It's OK,' I said to the ducks, tore up the bread, and tossed it in the water. I folded the wet plastic, put it in my pocket.

I was always cleaning up after him.

I sat on a rock, aching for my father. But with the ache, I felt lighter and older. I always thought I'd have a permanent broken part in me because of the problems with my dad. Now I see that it isn't the problems along the way that make us or break us. It's how we learn to stand and face them that makes the difference.

I squared my shoulders; heard a rustle in the bushes. A scared baby duck stuck his head out, gave a little quack.

I had one piece of bread left. I held it out for him.

He waddled out, unsure.

'Go for it,' I said. 'Make me proud.'

I threw the bread in the water. He dove in after it, raced past the other ducklings, gobbled it up.

Daring Duck Beats Odds to Win.

Another true survivor.

Like me.

Squashed

An all-American love story – and not just about pumpkins.

You can forget about a whizz-bang social life if, like Ellie Morgan, your greatest ambition is to grow a world class giant pumpkin.

Ellie has just forty-six days to boost her Big Max to legendary proportions and beat the reigning champion, the despicable Cyril Pool, in the Rock River Pumpkin Weigh-In. She needs all her courage and ingenuity to battle against rain, frost, bugs, fungus and pumpkin thieves – especially when helping her to protect Big Max seems to have knocked out Wes, the new boy in town, just when Ellie needs him most.

'an intriguing and poignant tale with a lot of humour.'
The Times

'Skillful plot development and strong characterization are real strengths here. Ellie's perceptive, intelligent and funny narrative keeps the story lively right up to its satisfying conclusion.' *School Library Journal*

Thwonk

'Never bring a cupid to school if you know what's good for you.'

Life for budding photographer A.J. would be just perfect if only high school heart-throb Peter Terris would notice her. So when a trainee cupid pops into her life, she doesn't hesitate. *Thwonk!* – and Peter is her devoted slave.

Only life isn't perfect – it's ghastly! Through a chaos of misunderstanding and bad feeling, A.J. realises it wasn't

Peter she wanted at all. Only now her elusive cupid has disappeared, and A.J. looks like being stuck with her horrible hunk for ever . . .

'This fine comic writer . . . has created . . . a Nineties heroine, who gets her life together through her career.' *Daily Telegraph*